**Low voices, mumbling yet lyrical. . .**

Desperately Priscilla fought against it—the shock, the fever, the uncertainties—until finally she relented. She needed these people who had befriended her, and if that meant placing her life in their hands, so be it. Soon Walkingstock would know she were ill if he didn't suspect already.

She opened her eyes, prepared to meet his, but the heavily lashed brown ones that stared at her were not the black eyes of Walkingstick. They were, however, familiar, as though she had seen those eyes in a dream, and she realized with a start that she had. But the rugged face attached—the comely face with its straight nose and jagged scar along one cheek—was one she didn't know.

"You're awake," said the well-molded lips, pressed thin. "Don't worry, Little Dove. You're in good hands."

She wasn't worried. Was she? At least she hadn't been until now.

# BEYOND THE SMOKY CURTAIN

*Mary Harwell Sayler*

Serenade/Saga
**BOOKS**
of the Zondervan Publishing House
Grand Rapids, Michigan

A NOTE FROM THE AUTHOR:

*I love to hear from my readers! You may correspond with me by writing:*

Mary Harwell Sayler
1415 Lake Drive, S.E.,
Grand Rapids, MI 49506

*Please include a stamped, self-addressed envelope if you would like a personal response. Thanks.*

BEYOND THE SMOKY CURTAIN
Copyright © 1985 by Mary Harwell Sayler
Grand Rapids, Michigan

Serenade/Saga is an imprint of Zondervan Publishing House,
1415 Lake Drive, S.E., Grand Rapids, Michigan 49506.

ISBN 0-310-46842-6

*Edited by Pamela M. Jewell*
*Designed by Kim Koning*

*Printed in the United States of America*

85  86  87  88  89  90  91  /  10  9  8  7  6  5  4  3  2  1

# FOREWORD

Dear Reader,

Historical research often means conflicting views,
and so it's necessary to find trustworthy sources. For
this book, mine were: The Museum of the Cherokee
in North Carolina, the Tennessee Historical Society,
and the Cherokee Historical Society in Oklahoma.

The resulting story is, of course, fiction, but one
"real" person does have a role–Nancy Ward, Nan-
ye-hi, best known perhaps as "Cherokee Rose." This
woman fascinated me because of her courage, her
social concerns, and her unbigoted attitudes during
her reign as the Beloved Woman of the nation.

And so, I dedicate this book to the beloved women
of *this* nation—the loving women who work to
communicate that love to their families, their neigh-
bors, and those people totally unlike themselves.

Special thanks to my uncle and aunt, Vernon and
Sara Angel, who pointed me in the right direction for

my research, and to my cousin, Martha Henegar, and her friend Claudia Gatewood, who took me in that direction—the Great Smoky Mountains.

*God's best to you,*
Mary Harwell Sayler
DeLand, Florida

## CHAPTER 1

BESIDE HER SOMEONE GROANED, then silence.

"Charles?"

The single word choked out on the little breath she had, and the velvety gray eyes, which she had almost opened, clamped tightly shut from the small exertion. She knew her husband needed help, but she could not lift a leaden finger from the rough log that had carried them both to shore.

Was Charles alive? If only she could turn her head . . . If only . . .

*"If only father were home, Priscilla Davis, you wouldn't be talking so foolishly!" her older sister, Lettie, exclaimed. Her long silk skirt swept the room with indignation. "I can't imagine what that frontiersman said to fill you and Charles with such a ridiculous notion."*

*"You'd understand if you'd been there," Priscilla injected.*

*"Hmmphf! As if I'd listen to a charlatan! What*

does this Jones person know of the savage unless he's one himself? And if he is so concerned for the spiritual welfare of the . . . the . . . ."

"Cherokee," Priscilla offered.

"Savages!" Lettie insisted. "Why isn't Mr. Jones among them himself instead of traveling about the Carolinas arousing the sympathies of romantic girls?"

Priscilla's full lips set in a thin line. "I may be nineteen, but I'm hardly a romantic, Lettie. Charles and I are prepared to face whatever hardships are required." Her dimpled chin tilted upward. "God has called us to serve Him among the Cherokee, and that's exactly what we shall do."

"Then Charles Prescott is as foolish as you are, Priscilla! Oh, don't look so stricken! I've known Charles all of his twenty-two years, but apparently I don't know him at all! I've thought of him as a brother, but never as a brother-in-law. Tell me, Priscilla, do you love him?"

"I'm fond of Charles. You know that."

"Fond!" Her sister mocked. "Will fondness sustain you when you bear his children—alone—in some primitive Indian village?"

"Lettie!" Priscilla exclaimed. Her ringless hands flew to her flushed throat.

But her sister continued unmercifully. "Good! I see I've gotten your attention. Perhaps Charles' family can shock some sense into him."

"It's pointless to discuss this, Lettie. I've quite made up my mind." Priscilla struggled to regain her composure. Then assuming a dignity she no longer felt, she rose from the striped, silk loveseat and rang a small, crystal bell.

8

*Lettie opened her mouth as if to speak, but the intended words pealed into laughter. "Oh, Priscilla, darling, whatever are you doing?"*

*"I'm ringing for tea," she said with a haughty lift of her dimple.*

*"Tea?" Lettie repeated amidst her own giggles. "And who, pray tell, will bring your tea when you're in that unnamed territory with your beloved savages?"*

*The crystal bell dropped, shattering against the oak-planked floor.*

An owl hooted. A twig snapped.

Her dry throat ached, but there was no bell to shatter the deepening quiet. No servants. No tea. No one to call.

"Charles?"

Priscilla's hand unloosed its hold on the log, her palm scraping on the rough bark as her arm fell heavily onto the wet grass. Something supported her other arm, something sodden and unmoving. A whimper, escaped her lips, and a shudder racked her thin body lying face down on the bank of the swollen river. The last time she'd laid her gray eyes on Charles, he'd been unconscious in her grasp as she'd kicked and struggled against the ragging water moving the log closer and closer to the shore.

She couldn't remember reaching her destination, but the grass cushioning her drenched, blond head assured her that she had. Muddied petticoats clung to her tattered stockings, and her linen shawl, still wrapped across her front and tied in the back, molded itself uncomfortably against her soggy bodice. Her water-logged shoes anchored her weary feet to the ground, and her head felt unbearably heavy.

9

She had to move, to stir. She had to find out. With tremendous effort, she arched her neck and scratched her face along the matted grasses until she'd upturned the other cheek. Her long lashes fluttered from weighted lids, and the slitted view confirmed what she had not wished to see. The still, sodden mass beneath her arm was Charles, and his round blue eyes were opened wide as if something had caught him by surprise.

Oh, Charles . . . Oh, Charles . . .

"Oh, Charles! My lovely gown is getting wet!" Priscilla exclaimed. "Do you suppose that's what Lettie meant when she said it's bad luck to marry on such a dreary day as this." She gave a little laugh, determined not to allow her spirits or her wedding day to be dampened despite the rain.

Charles extended a gloved hand to help his new bride into the Prescott family's carriage. "That's superstitious talk, Priscilla," Charles rebuked her mildly. "We mustn't concern ourselves with trivial matters."

Trivial? For a moment resentment flared that he should think their marriage insignificant in any way, even regarding omens. It wasn't every day that a girl married, and conventional or not, Priscilla wanted to enjoy it. Her lower lip protruded slightly as she bunched together her white, satin skirt to make room for her new husband. But, seating himself, Charles took no note of her hurt feelings.

Priscilla stole a sidewards glance. Charles eyes glistened with suppressed excitement, and she knew his thoughts lay ahead as hers often did—miles ahead towards the unnamed, reclaimed territory over the Appalachians and beyond the smoky curtain of civilization.

The king forbade settlement west of the mountains a decade ago when the warring French finally gave up their claims, and that was odd, Priscilla thought. Until the French stirred up trouble among the Cherokee, the people generally accepted the British colonists who had settled on the ancestral mountain lands. But the French had wanted the territory for themselves, and so they had armed the Indians with guns and grudges. Then, after a long fight, France relinquished all claims in North America, and in that same year, 1763, the English king said it was too dangerous for colonists to settle beyond the mountains. Strange! Yet Priscilla supposed his highness had lost too many soldiers and too many sleepless nights to concern himself further with the safety of colonial adventurers.

That was ten years ago, and as far as Priscilla knew the king's order was, at first, obeyed. But in recent years, a number of families had drifted into the area, and most had settled near the Watauga River. Last year, 1772, the group banded together to form the Watauga Association, and their elected government was the first organized west of the Alleghenies. Law and order, the Rev. Jones had assured her and Charles.

Priscilla had her doubts. It wasn't that she disbelieved the good reverend but, as much as she hated to admit it, Lettie had a point when she said that, coming from the Carolina territory, the reverend's sense of law and order was probably quite remote from their own.

What did reassure Priscilla, however, was the fact that the people of the Watauga Association leased the land from the Cherokee. Surely that meant the

11

strained relationships had been mended. A promising sign, indeed.

Priscilla sighed. She wished that her relationships with her family were not equally strained. Lettie's sensibilities were in such a state of war that she had refused to come to the wedding altogether. Mama couldn't, of course, being too much the invalid, in and out of her own little world. And Papa, as usual, was off somewhere in England, trying to gain favors from the king. He would probably succeed, increasing their already impressive wealth and landholdings in the process. Poor Papa. He had little else but properties and pleasant titles.

Ironically, Priscilla thought herself the greedy one! She wanted so much more than her parents or her sister had. She wanted to be wanted, to be needed— to serve, to count. And how blessed she felt that Charles, who was from a family not unlike hers, wanted the same. God Himself was calling!

Calling . . .

"Charles? Charles?"

Slowly, steadily, her voice rose from a whisper. "Charles!" she screamed, and the awful sound wailed deep within the forest. Again and again, his name came in a groan from her lips, from her throat, from her heart as she nudged him, shook him, pounded him with impotent fists. At last, she closed his stunned eyes with her small hands and laid her blond head on his unmoving chest.

*"Don't, Priscilla!" he had said that first night of their travels when she, a new bride, had sought his chest for a pillow.*

*She had raised her head to look at him, but his pensive eyes stared off into the dark.*

*"Is—is something wrong?"* she had asked, suddenly shy.

*"No!"* The word snapped as he thrust her away
from him to sit upright by the fire. *"Priscilla, I must
think of the consequences of—of lying so close to
you."*

*"But, Charles, we're married!"*

*"Yes, we are, and I thank God you're my wife.
You're lovely, Priscilla, but you must understand
. . . ."* He turned to her with another passion lighting
his eyes. *"God has called us! Just think of it! Yet
we're going into an untamed land to bring His name
to the savages, and our very lives may be endangered
for it. I dare not make you more vulnerable, Priscilla,"* he added gently. *"Nor will I risk the precious,
innocent life of an unborn child. We must wait until
we've made friends of the Indians and the settlers.
Then, my dearest, you'll not be able to keep me from
your lovely arms."*

*As a pledge of things to come, Charles had sealed
his promise with a searing kiss.*

She kissed him now. Lightly, gently, finally.

A virgin widow, Priscilla struggled to her feet,
hearing Lettie's "I told you so" in the unearthly
quiet. She pushed the comfortless thought away as
best she could and surveyed the scene at hand. Her
husband was dead. The horses were gone. And she
had not a dry stitch to her name.

"Oh, God. Oh, God!" she sobbed. "What do I do
now?"

*"Good grief, Priscilla! Don't you know how to do
anything well?"* Charles asked with uncharacteristic
exasperation. *She'd burned the johnnycake for the
third night in a row, and the squirrel, which Charles*

13

had used entirely too much ammunition to shoot, wasn't cooked through. He flung his pewter plate down in disgust, and she hurried to scoop the precious meat from the ground. With a little water and a stew pot, tomorrow night's dinner might be intact.

Using conversation to distract him from what she was doing, Priscilla said quietly, "I'm doing the best I can, Charles." Then she pressed her lips together to refrain from saying how much he was beginning to sound like Lettie.

To her surprise, her husband laid a tender hand on her thin shoulder. "I know you are, Priscilla," he signed. "I suppose we've much to learn, but we've been traveling nigh onto two fortnights. I say! We've done remarkably well."

"Only a month, Charles?" Somehow it seemed much longer since they'd left civilization behind. "And we've passed so few cabins." Without the assistance of those settlers, however, she doubted they'd have gotten this far.

"It's desolate country," Charles agreed, "without even a familiar songbird to cheer us on."

"Why is that?" Priscilla wondered. How she'd come to hate the unnerving quiet.

"Food, I imagine. The forest floor is too thick with oak leaves and pine needles to allow any grass to poke through, and without it, there's no seed for songbirds, or, for that matter, no grass for the deer."

Steathily, Priscilla wrapped the tough squirrel meat in her handkerchief and stuck it in her pocket. "What about us, Charles? Did we bring enough supplies?

"If not, the Lord will provide."

Priscilla gave her pocket a pat. "But, Charles, we

14

*can't expect God to provide for our own negligence. He gave us good sense too, and surely, He expects us to use it."* Now, she was sounding like Lettie, she realized, to her chagrin.

But Charles' thoughts had wandered dreamily into the green cavern of a forest.

*"Soon, Priscilla, we'll cross that shining river we glimpsed from higher peaks. And then . . ."*

*"Yes, Charles?"*

*"And then it won't be long until we reach our promised land."*

The words now seemed prophetic, for surely Charles had reached his.

Left behind, Priscilla stared at him, willing him to move. He didn't, and she shook her head, trying to waken herself from this haze in which she'd been ever since the flooded waters overtook her. Gradually an apathetic sort of energy restored itself, and her head cleared. Charles was dead, and she must bury him.

How?

Priscilla squinted into the darkening forest that even earlier in the noonday light had seemed oppressive and gloomy. Soon the blackness of evening would extinguish all light, and she had no flint, no fire, no food, no husband. She hoped that Charles would be right—that God would provide. But—frankly, she couldn't see how.

Dragging herself to her husband's body, Priscilla felt a strange detachment from the situation, from what she knew she had to do. With no tools, no supplies, there was no way to dig a proper grave, and she hadn't the strength anyway. She had considered looking for one of the caves they had discovered occasionally in the outcropping of rock, but it would be dark soon. And, she reminded herself, she had no flint with which to start a fire. Animals prowled those caves in which she and Charles had taken shelter, but with a protecting blaze and Charles beside her, she had been unafraid before.

Now her hands trembled as she gathered a mound of stones and placed them in the outspread jacket that she had removed from Charles' still form. She thanked God that he had discarded his gentlemanly attire before leaving home, replacing it with the sturdy leather coat often worn by the frontiersman. The fringed jacket would serve well for her purposes, and so would the river which had taken her husband's life.

When she had gathered enough stones to outweigh Charles' slender frame, Priscilla tied the sleeves of the jacket and belted the loose ends together. Then she secured the apparatus tightly around her husband's middle, and with a mighty heave, she shoved him into the river. She had done her work well. The body sank rapidly out of sight.

Priscilla stared at it until her velvety eyes glazed. How easy it would be to slip into the water. How easy to slide in and out of the tormented, unreal world that only her mother had known. But a wave of nausea spurred her to action, to fight the heavings of her own emotions.

Around her, the forest was a verdant tomb, and she yelled angrily into the silence. "You'll not have me yet!"

Something stirred. She was sure of it. One of the horses perhaps.

On that hopeful note, Priscilla clicked her tongue, but there was no responding whinny, no gentle thud of hooves on the carpeted floor of the woods.

"Hello! Is someone there?" she called into the monstrous quiet.

An owl hooted. Then another. And then the boy appeared.

He stepped soundlessly from behind the massive trunk of a tulip poplar, and stood staring at her with enormous brown eyes.

Priscilla stared back. What lovely skin he had! Perhaps it was the eerie light of the forest, but the boy looked to be made of olives or berries, glistening with oil or dew.

"Don't be afraid," she said, feeling remarkably calm herself. Just knowing that there was indeed another human being alive in these woods had somehow made all the difference.

It occurred to her then that this young man might not speak her language, and if not, she certainly didn't know his. She had to communicate; she had to make him understand that she was harmless and alone. And she had to do so quickly, for he looked as though he might bolt at any moment.

"Please," she said softly, "don't go. I need your help." And whether or not he could comprehend her words, she felt certain that her tone of voice would convey her attitude of peace.

She smiled then and held out both hands, palms up, to show him that she was friendly and empty and alone. His own face remained inquisitive, solemn, but when she continued to stand there, unmoving, his expression cleared, and he gave a single nod.

With a pendulum sweep of his hand, he beckoned her to follow. And, of course, she did without a backward look. Charles was gone – dead without even a glimpse of the Cherokees. And she, Priscilla

17

Prescott, had no choice but to go ahead into this new territory with a young Indian boy for her guide.

## CHAPTER 2

THEY WALKED FOREVER.

Occasionally the boy would pause to select a plant or pluck a leaf or dig a root. Then he'd deposit his find in a leather pouch that swung down from his waist. He never smiled, but Priscilla had the impression that he was pleased with each discovery. Though why a dirty root or broken twig was significant, she didn't know.

Continuously, the boy's large eyes swept the forest floor, the brush, the trees, yet his gaze avoided her watchful stare. Except for her brief inspections of the dwindling soles of her wet walking shoes, Priscilla dared not take her own eyes from him.

This mere child of ten, eleven perhaps, was her only hope of survival. Oh, what would Lettie say to that! Thank goodness she didn't know, might never know, Priscilla reminded herself. And besides, her real hope was in the Lord. He was the One who had brought here here, and He was the One who would provide.

Except for Charles. What about Charles? Why had God not provided for him?

Perhaps He had, she told herself, as she hurried to keep pace with the tireless strides of the child. God's almighty view was not limited to the material, to the confining matter of a body, and even though her own body grew wearier with each step, Priscilla was not one to question His all-knowing, all-seeing perspective.

She'd thought it would be dark by now, and, indeed, the greens and pinks and browns of the woods had begun to gray. What would she do if the boy strode into the night, intent on his own mysterious purposes, his own destination? How could she keep track of him then? Odd, but her own destination did not trouble her for the moment. She simply did not want to be left alone in the blackening night.

Overhead, a tangle of oak branches charred in the dusk, and Priscilla gave a little shudder. Involuntarily her steps had slowed until her scraps of shoes plowed small furrows in the forest bed. The cooling air penetrated her still damp clothing, so her linen shawl brought no comfort from the chill. Intermittently, her heavy skirts fastened upon briars and twigs until persistent vines snatched and tugged her down. She fell upon the earth, her gloveless hands too limp to catch her, and she lay there, breathless, but struggling to get up.

Apparently the thud of her fall had alerted her young guide, for the boy scrambled back in her direction.

" *A ni si di* ," he said when he'd freed her of the clutching vine.

"Thank you." Priscilla managed a wan smile.

"Would you help me up, please?" She shifted her weight and held out her hand, hoping the gesture would communicate her need. But the boy stood above her, shaking his head.

" *A ni si di* ," he repeated, and then to show her, he dropped onto the ground, arranging the leaves and himself in a position for sleeping.

*A ni si di, a place to lie down*, he was telling her, but when he hopped up and started off, panic goaded Priscilla into action.

"Don't leave! Please," she called, and in any language, the fear in her voice was unmistakable.

The boy hesitated in a half-turn while Priscilla tried, unsuccessfully, to rise to her feet.

"I can keep up; I can manage," she said to herself more than to him, but her jellied limbs refused to comply. She sank back wearily while keeping her eyes steadily fastened on the child.

He seemed to be trying to tell her something, but all she could comprehend was that he wanted her to stay put, which was the last thing she herself had in mind.

"Don't go! Don't leave me here!" she begged again. "Yes. Yes. I know I need to rest, but how can I if you leave? You might not come back! You might leave me here to die alone! Charles is gone. Don't you understand? My husband is gone!" But the boy was going, too, and there was nothing Priscilla could do to stop him.

"Oh, God! Oh, God!" she cried. "Don't You leave me! Please," she ended on a groan, and her head bowed in exhaustion and defeat.

She didn't see, then, that the boy retraced his steps until the breath of his presence stirred her.

" *Ha wa* ," the child said, as though letting her

21

know everything was all right. Quickly he unfastened the leather pouch from his waist and pressed it into Priscilla's hand. Then with the bounding grace of a deer, he dashed into the black stillness of the forest.

He would be back, she told herself. Whatever woodsy concoction the pouch contained, it was important to the child, yet he'd placed it in her hands, a pledge. He would be back for the pouch, for her, and with that tender promise held tightly to her bosom, Priscilla slipped into her own black stillness.

Other pledges overtook her rest as she dreamed of lying in Charles' arms, of holding him and being held, but cold fingers of reality shook her pleasant sleep. She shivered against the night air embracing her, and held only the little pouch against her heart for warmth. He would be back. He would be back.

"Charles?"

Someone tugged at the leather pocket clutched against her, and Priscilla rolled over onto it, unable to do more to protect it or herself.

" *Ha wa* ." The child's voice sighed. " *Ga-tli-ha* ."

Relief softened the brittle edges of fatigue, and Priscilla slept as bidden.


A gentle nudge woke Priscilla with the first greening of the morn, and she cried out in joy when she saw the boy standing over her. So, she had not dreamed his return after all! Gingerly, she raised herself on a tattered sleeve and pushed back the blankets which the boy had apparently placed over her during the night. The precious pouch swung once more from his waist, but it was not that movement which startled her.

Beside the dying fire, an old man squatted, staring

22

at her with sunken, black eyes. His wrinkled skin suggested advanced age, but no sag corresponded in his erect posture, and he looked as though he'd been carved and polished from the straightest oak. He neither smiled nor frowned, and Priscilla, not knowing what to make of him, looked away to the familiar face of the boy.

*"Tsa du li ha tsu ga-du?"* the child asked, gesturing toward the fire.

Not wishing to move her aching body just yet nor place herself closer to the ancient man who guarded the glowing embers, Priscilla shook her head.

"No, thank you. I'm quite warm," she said, giving her blanketed shoulder a rub. "You've been good to me. I wish I could make you understand how grateful I am."

*"Tsa du li ha tsu ga-du?"* the boy repeated. "Ga-du. Ga-du." He offered up something yellow-brown and presumably edible.

"Bread," the old man confirmed it. "He asks if you want bread."

"You speak English!" Priscilla exclaimed, delighted, for she was as hungry for recognizable sounds as she was for food. But the old man did not respond further until she'd nibbled the last tasteless crumb of ga-du, and even then, she realized that any conversation would require her probe.

"Are . . . are you Cherokee?" she asked, hoping it didn't sound rude.

The old man nodded. *"Aniyv-wiya.* Principal People."

Priscilla wasn't certain if she'd received an affirmative or not. Struggling into a position of greater dignity, she sipped the tea, a strange hot concoction which the boy had offered.

"I am Priscilla Prescott, and I'm recently widowed, sir, but my husband and I were, uh, looking for the Cherokee."

"You found."

Priscilla sighed her relief. Not only had she found the people for whom she searched, but she'd been spared the question of why she was looking in the first place. Explaining could be awkward, and she still felt too weak to have her full wits about her. Another night's sleep might help, and perhaps another cup of that unusual tea.

She'd begun to extend the hollowed gourd for replenishment when the old man rose with surprising agility.

"We go now."

"But—but, sir! I don't even know where we're going or who you are or . . ." She stammered to a stop, unsure how to express her curiosity in a manner that would not offend.

A gnarled finger pointed to the boy. "He is Little Spoon. I am Walkingstick, Medicine Man of Chota."

A medicine man! Then the boy must be a helper, an apprentice of sorts, Priscilla realized. No wonder he'd been so fascinated with certain plants and roots. And the tea! Undoubtedly it did have medicinal properties for she felt remarkably better.

Slowly she rose to her feet that seemed ready now to hold her.

"Chota," she repeated, questioning. "Is that the place where you live?"

Again the man nodded. "It is home of the Principal Chiefs. Home of the Beloved Woman."

Beloved Woman. She turned the phrase over in her mind then stored it away for another time.

"And—and you'll take me there? To Chota?" Priscilla asked hopefully.

This time, however, the old man shook his head. "We come to smaller village first. There, Bear Claw will find you."

"I'm sorry. I don't understand."

"You look for Cherokee. Bear Claw looks for new wife. Even Little Spoon knows it is good."

"But—but—" Priscilla's protest went no further for Walkingstick terminated the conversation by setting off down an incline that immediately swallowed him from sight.

Perhaps, she comforted herself, she had misunderstood. But perhaps not. It appeared now that the boy, Little Spoon, had befriended her for a reason—to provide this man named Bear Claw with a wife.

"See! Savages!" she could almost hear Lettie say. But, no. Her treatment thus far had been quite courteous and no more primitive than the conditions under which she and Charles had traveled. She had no desire, of course, for anyone to force her hand in marriage, but had that not been her own father's intent?

Poor Papa, she thought now, remembering with discomfort the harsh words which had passed between them prior to his last trip to England.

"I shall find a suitable young man for you, Priscilla, while I'm away. Lord Chaucey perhaps, or someone equally marriageable."

She'd stomped her slender foot to no avail. "Find someone for Lettie if you will, sir. But not for me."

Even now she could see his handsome face distorted in black fury. "You are my daughter, Priscilla Davis, and you shall do as I say. Let there not be another word on this subject." And there wasn't. Nor would there be now.

Lord Chaucey. Bear Claw. What difference did it make? At the moment, her primary concern was simply to place one ragged shoe in front of another, a feat she found increasingly difficult to do.

The vigor of a night's rest and a morning's refreshment had dissipated all too quickly, and Priscilla feared she couldn't travel much further. Twice Little Spoon had had to retrace his steps when she had stumbled, and both times they had scarcely been out of the night's camp. Now, however, he stopped of his own accord, dropping to his knees on the cool, damp earth.

Gratefully, Priscilla leaned against the smooth trunk of a tulip poplar, watching the boy as she caught her breath. Her keen sight took in every movement with special interest now that she knew what business he was about, but even so, his actions astonished her.

As he searched for a particular species of plant, Little Spoon seemed to count off the first three before taking the fourth. He did not take the plant, however, until he'd spoken to it in a prayer-like way, and Priscilla had the impression that the boy was asking the plant's permission to uproot it. He then carefully dug the tender roots and shoots, and when that task was finished, he dropped a bead in, an offering of thanksgiving, before recovering the hole.

Something told Priscilla that Little Spoon had forgotten her presence and that her watchful stare would be an intrusion. Before he'd noticed her once more, she turned her head away and closed her eyes.

She could have slept, standing there, but the boy's voice beckoned.

*"E gv yi,"* he said, his gesture indicating, "You go first."

Since they had been following a deer path, Priscilla had no trouble obeying, although she walked twice as far, staggering from side to side along the way. Fortunately, however, the downhill slopes had leveled, and with a final descent, she came upon a small creek that was enlarged with the earlier spring rains.

Walkingstick was waiting. Having gone ahead of them, he had packed up the blanket rolls and scant supplies and loaded them into a canoe.

*"U s qua lv hv,"* he said. "It is ready."

Had she possessed the energy, Priscilla would have given a little dance for joy. The grandeur of the Prescott family carriage could not compare with the beautiful sight of this rough dug-out, and with thanks to God, she seated herself on the flat bottom of yellow pine.

*Oh, Lord, how good are your provisions!* she prayed silently as they slipped without a splash into the water.

With nothing more required of her but rest, Priscilla settled into a semi-reclining position that offered her a brilliant view of the sky. During these many weeks of journey, she'd seldom seen anything but leaf and limb and her own two feet, usually atangle. But now the trees parted at the widest span of the stream, and silky strips of blue peeked through the ever-present green. Her eyes could feast forever, she thought, but a spring breeze whispered and the water gently rocked until the conspiring sound and motion soon lulled her to sleep.

At first her mind drifted as peacefully as the canoe that rested securely upon the water. But Charles' death and the loss of small, but precious items in the river along with all of the supplies, helped contribute to Priscilla's exhaustion and uncertain future. She dreamed she, too, was drowning. Then, rescued at the last minute by the claws of a bear, she awoke with a whimper.

Sometime during her nap, Walkingstick and Little Spoon had changed positions so that the boy now guided the small dugout around large, smooth stones and exposed tree roots. From his vantage point, the old man kept a practiced eye on Priscilla which she found so unnerving that she closed her own heavy lids. She preferred to stay awake, to sort her thoughts until she could ask Walkingstick the most pressing questions that concerned her. Thus far, his short responses had led her to believe that he would not welcome idle chatter or foolish questions, and it was increasingly difficult to separate logic from nonsense.

She supposed she had a fever. If so, she prayed that she could hide it, for she certainly didn't want to be exposed to the strange practices of a medicine man. Charles would not like it. Lettie would not like it. Papa would not like it.

Masks. There would be masks to ward away the evil spirits. And chants. Chants to contact the higher powers, the spirits of good. There would be shakers, hissing and rattling, warning like a snake trapped in a smoke-filled hut.

Fire. Blazing fire, smouldering fire. And the smell of herbs and the taste of bitter brew.

Poultices, heavy and hot. Cool hands on the forehead. Chilling water to sponge away the dirt, the fears, the memories.

Low voices, mumbling yet lyrical. Frowns. And

28

eyes. Dark eyes, deep cavernous eyes, mystical eyes that drew and tugged one back to life.

Desperately Priscilla fought against it—the shock, the fever, the uncertainties—until finally she relented. She needed these people who had befriended her, and if that meant placing her life in their hands, so be it. Soon Walkingstock would know she were ill if he didn't suspect already. It was foolish to try to hide that fact when she did indeed need his help.

She opened her eyes, prepared to meet his, but the heavily lashed brown ones that stared at her were not the black eyes of Walkingstick. They were, however, familiar, as though she had seen those eyes in a dream, and she realized with a start that she had. But the rugged face attached—the comely face with its straight nose and jagged scar along one cheek—was one she didn't know.

"You're awake," said the well-molded lips, pressed thin. "Don't worry, Little Dove. You're in good hands."

She wasn't worried. Was she? At least she hadn't been until now. She tried to speak, but the questions stuck on a thatched tongue.

Where was she? Where were Walkingstick and Little Spoon? And who was this tall and arrogantly comfortable white man who stood over her as though they were old friends?

Priscilla snapped her eyelids shut. Obviously, she was much sicker than she thought.

## CHAPTER 3

"OH, NO, YOU DON'T! Mrs. Prescott! Priscilla Prescott!
Wake up!"

That man, that insufferably rude and disquietingly
handsome man was shaking her by the shoulders!
Priscilla whacked his hands away.

'Sir!'' she found her voice at last. "Have you taken
leave of your senses?''

"I thought *you* had," he answered. "Sorry, but you
have given me a few sleepless nights, you know."

"I know no such thing. I've never seen you before
today, so sleepless nights on my account are highly
unlikely.'' She gave him what she hoped was a
scathing look to put him in his place. "Now if you'll
please get out of my—my . . ." What? Canoe? Not
anymore. Hut? It was that, it seemed, but it wasn't
hers. "Bedchamber," she finished grandly.

A quick look around had proved her to be on a
blanketed shelf that was fastened to the wall as were
others around the hut. A thin leather veil separated

each sleeping cubicle, but someone—this man, no doubt—had pushed hers aside. And now he stood there, grinning broadly.

"If you please, sir, I'd like to rest." Except for a snort over her use of the word "bedchamber", he'd failed to move one bit. "I'm ill, assuming you hadn't noticed."

"On the contrary, Mourning Dove."

His possessive glance failed to reassure her as she realized that she no longer wore her tattered dress nor linen shawl. Someone had bathed her and redressed her in a loose-fitting garment. Someone had washed and combed her hair that now lay about her shoulders.

The crude implication of his stare brought heat to her cheeks.

"Set your mind at rest, madam. I have not had the pleasure of tending you myself. You'll have to thank Straw Basket for that. At any rate, you look much improved."

Priscilla was inclined to disagree. "I told you, sir, I'm ill. And I don't know where I am or who Straw Basket is, and I especially do not know you, sir."

"That's an improvement. For the last few nights, you didn't know who you were yourself."

"Oh." Actually, it was a comfort to know that she was on the mend instead of the decline. But Priscilla didn't care to give this man the satisfaction of that acknowledgement.

Suddenly he gave a low bow, clicking his heels together as if to show that he'd had proper manners at some time in his life.

"Permit me to introduce myself," he said in such a courtly fashion that Priscilla had no doubts he was mocking her. "My name is Garth Daniels, son of Lord Richard and Lady Elizabeth Daniels from the colony of Virginia."

"Virginia! Then what on earth are you doing *wherever* we are?" she blurted.

Mr. Daniels threw back his dark head, laughing. "I might ask you the same, Madam, but I'll not tax you now. Shortly put, I'm here because I want to be. I trade goods between Indians and whites, and keep the peace as best I can."

"How very noble of you," Priscilla remarked crisply. This man seemed so self-assured, so cocky, that she wanted to set him down a peg. "I should think, sir, that it would be difficult to help keep the peace when you lack simple courtesy and tact."

Instead of being set down, however, Mr. Daniels' temper rose. "You'd better get something straight, little lady, if you want to survive long in this territory. The etiquette you know won't win any ribbons or beaux. Keep it honest; keep it kind, and you might keep that pretty little scalp."

Her blond hair prickled at the suggestion, but Priscilla, at last, had her wish. Without another word, Garth Daniels took his leave.

As soon as he had gone, Priscilla wished he hadn't. Insufferable though the man was, he could be valuable to her. She still had no idea where she was or how she had gotten here except to guess that Walkingstick and Little Spoon had deposited her at the small village near Chota as planned. But now that she was here, what was she to do without an interpreter? She hadn't considered such matters when Charles was alive.

But Charles was dead.

The realization hit her anew, overwhelming her

with grief until she thought her waking was more nightmarish than her sleep. What grotesque dreams she had had. Only now she realized that most of them were real. The eerie chants, the bitter potions, the acrid smells, the not-quite-human masks waving in nose-down designs—all of it had probably occurred right here in this hut.

Was this dismaying world what God had called her to? And if so, what did He expect her to do about it? She had given it no thought until now, having instead some vague notion of immediate acceptance among the Cherokee who would come to her with all sorts of spiritual ills. She had seen herself surrounded by groups of loving children, eager for their Bible lessons while Charles taught the adults, instructing them in the ways of God. *How* she and Charles would accomplish those feats had not been clear.

She wished Charles were here to advise her about the language barrier, the cultural differences, the weakened condition of her own body. But Priscilla supposed it didn't matter what Charles would or wouldn't have done anyway. She, too, had been called, and it was up to God Himself to guide her in what He would have her do.

She tried to place herself in a prayerful state of mind to concentrate on His will, but the dreadful pounding inside her head interfered.

*Kaboom. Kaboom. Kaboom.*

The constant thudding assaulted her ears until Priscilla realized that the noise came from without rather than from within. Seeking the source, she arose from her bedshelf, but a wave of dizziness thrust her back between the covers.

"*U yo i!*" A young woman cautioned from the doorway.

Having discovered already that it was not wise for her to get up yet, Priscilla studied the squat figure. The woman, a girl really, had that same beautiful skin as Little Spoon and eyes like shiny black buttons. Her simple dress, woven of hemp, dyed red and black, was similar to the one that Priscilla wore, but the Indian girl's garment was caught about her thick waist with a fringed and beaded sash. Deerskin covered her feet and rose to meet her skirt at the knees so that when she walked, there was no sound. No swishing skirt. No thumping heels on the dirt-packed floor.

"Are you Straw Basket?" Priscilla asked, slowly raising herself on an elbow.

The girl nodded, grinning shyly.

"Then you're the one to thank for taking care of me. Oh." Priscilla stopped, aware of the puzzlement creeping over the girl's face. "You don't understand me, do you? Oh, dear. I did so want to tell you how much I appreciate your help."

"*Wa-do.*" Garth Daniels voice came through the entrance of the hut, and Priscilla gave a dizzying start. "*Wa-do* means thank you."

"*Wa-do,*" Priscilla mimicked. "*Wa-do,* Straw Basket."

"You're welcome," Daniels injected.

"I thought you had gone!"

"I had." He flashed a smile that Priscilla found annoying. "Gone to fetch your gracious hostess so you two could be *properly* introduced."

"Does she live here alone?"

Daniels shook his head. "This is her parents' house. When she's married, she'll have her own."

Priscilla raised herself a bit higher. "How can she tolerate it?" she whispered, as though Straw Basket might understand.

Daniels shot her a harsh glance. "Since you're obviously accustomed to a grand estate, I assume you mean the size, the crudity of this place."

"I mean no such thing, sir. I was refering to that awful noise. How can she bear being so close to it?"

Daniels' frown eased. "That noise is everywhere. It's the sound of the women throughout the village pounding the day's corn. You'll get used to it in time, Mourning Dove, and other unique sounds and sights too, I pray." When he spoke softly like that, he seemed to be another man.

"Why do you call me Mourning Dove?" Priscilla asked.

"It suits you, does it not? I understand you are in mourning. And, your eyes are as gray as the feathers of a mourning dove. Besides," he added, "it's the name Walkingstick gave you, and I don't argue with him."

"Do you only argue with widows confined to their beds, Mr. Daniels?"

"Ah, madam, that is a predicament that time will surely resolve," he said, and Priscilla didn't know to which he referred—her widowed state or her current confinement. Either way, she felt embarrassed.

"Incidentally," he went on, 'there is no need for formality here. You may call me Garth." His dark eyes took on an impish gleam. "And I will call you Priscilla. Or Prissy."

"Certainly not!" Regardless of this man's reasons or preferences, Priscilla did not care to have him call her by her first name. And 'Prissy' had always irritated her—especially when said in the tone of voice Garth Daniels used.

"Then Mourning Dove it is—for now." He gave the bedshelf a thump.

"What do you mean, for now?" Priscilla clasped the fluttering heartbeat in her throat. Was she not going to be around much longer?

Daniels snickered. "Names have a way of changing among the Aniyv wiya. Take Straw Basket, for instance." He beckoned to the girl who had been stirring the fire in the middle of the dirt floor. Then he spoke to her in her native tongue.

Straw Basket answered, but her hands provided Priscilla with the only clue. First they rounded about her face, then gestured in a stroking motion, neither of which meant a thing to Priscilla.

Garth nodded, understanding. "She says her name was Little Moon as a child because of her round face. Then she became Painted Rock when she expressed her artistry by dabbing paint on every unturned stone. Now she weaves baskets of straw, and, I might add, they're the sturdiest and most attractive baskets made in the village."

Priscilla gave a little clap. "Then 'Straw Basket' denotes her occupation, like some of our English names—Baker, Carpenter, Smith."

"That's partly right," Garth said, "though every woman in the village fashions her own baskets when she has need. Also, 'Straw Basket' is a given name, showing character or special skill. But, in our culture, her last name would be Wolf. Her mother's family is part of the Wolf clan. There are seven clans in all." Suddenly he stopped. "Forgive me if I've tired you." He swept a low bow. "May I present Straw Basket? And, Straw Basket, Mourning Dove."

The younger girl giggled, and Priscilla couldn't help but smile. Laughter, it seemed, was the same in any language.

With Garth functioning as interpreter, Straw Basket expressed her gladness over Priscilla's improved health and welcomed her into the family home. Then, shyly, she added, *"I-gi-do."*

"Sister," Garth explained. "She invites you to become the sister she has lost."

His tone held no emotion, but Priscilla was deeply touched. "Tell her I would be most happy to have her for my sister."

"Perhaps," he replied, "you should tell her yourself."

"Perhaps I should," she answered tartly. Then turning to the girl, Priscilla gave her her warmest smile. *"I-gi-do,"* she said, then added, *"wa-do."*

Straw basket beamed, *"I-gi-do,"* she repeated, but the rest of her conversation was lost until Garth translated.

"She says you must have nourishment to recover your strength, and I quite agree. Would you take some soup?"

Priscilla nodded. *"Wa-do,* Straw Basket."

*"Tsa du li ha tsu ga-du?"* the girl asked, and when Garth began to interpret, Priscilla waved an impatient hand.

"I know! She asks if I want bread." She nodded in the affirmative, feeling rather pleased with herself. "Yes, Straw Basket. *Wa-do."*

Garth folded his arms high across his broad chest and gave Priscilla a look of approval.

"I don't suppose I need to tell you to eat lightly for a while?"

"Thank you, no."

"You'll have a varied diet here," Garth went on, unabashed, "wild game, fruits, vegetables, mushrooms, and nuts in season. But don't expect to sample plum pudding or chocolate bon bons."

"Really, Mr. Daniels . . ."

"Garth."

"Garth, then. You must think me a simpleton."

He shrugged. "Is anyone wise until experience teaches?"

Since she had no real answer, Priscilla changed the subject. "Tell me about Straw Basket's family— especially her sister."

To her surprise, however, Garth shook his head. "Another time. At the moment, you need food and rest more than information, and I have other matters to which I must attend." He gave a light bow. "Rest assured, madam, you've not seen the last of me."

Priscilla didn't know if that reassured her or not. But as soon as Garth was gone, she realized how very tired she was. Odd, how she hadn't noticed until now.

Sinking back wearily on her mattress of corn husks, Priscilla watched Straw Basket busy herself around the fire. Unlike the Davises' home, which had a kitchen set apart for safety's sake, this modest hut centered around the open flame. A hole in the domed roof allowed the smoke to escape, though much of it lingered in the sleeping cubicles and drifted, fog-like, about the room.

A patch of sunny sky covered the vent-hole, allowing Priscilla to glimpse the daylight, but, for the most part, the room was dark with its narrow-cut door and mud-plastered walls. The effect was not dreary, however, since woven baskets and straw mats and colorful clay pots of varying sizes hung about, brightening the interior.

Priscilla judged the one-room hut to be thirty feet

38

across. Back home, her bedroom was twenty-feet square, as were most of the rooms in the Davises' house.

At this very moment, Lettie would probably be in the music room, Mama on the sun porch, and Papa in his study—assuming that he was yet home. If not, Mama would be abed, wrapped in a dark velvet cocoon.

*I have to get up!* Priscilla thought, as a thread of panic spun itself around her. One could not serve or count or be needed when stuck away on a bedshelf! But thrashing about only succeeded in gaining Straw Basket's attention.

The girl said something that Priscilla could not understand, yet the soft flow of musical words soothed her, and she ceased her struggle against the heavy blanket. Food. Yes, that was what she needed. That would help.

She watched and waited as Straw Basket dipped a hollowed-out gourd into a clay pot that sat near the fire. Then the girl ladled the pottage into a small wooden bowl and brought it to Priscilla.

*"U-ga-ma."* Straw Basket pointed to the soup.

*"U-ga-ma.* Soup."

Straw Basket nodded. "Soo-oop," she said, and they both laughed.

For a few moments, the young women took turns identifying objects in their native languages, giggling over the foreign sounds they made. Then, rather sternly, Straw Basket said, *"Hi-ga."*

Not comprehending, Priscilla frowned. *"Hi-ga?"*

*"Hi-ga,"* Straw Basket insisted. She made movements with her hands and mouth, reminding Priscilla to eat.

39

Obediently, she complied, making use of the plain wooden spoon that Straw Basket gave her. How light it felt—not at all like the heavy, ornately scrolled silverware to which she was accustomed. But the wooden spoon and bowl stirred a memory, and so did the soup with its beans and corn and chunks of squash, floating in a thick broth.

She couldn't have been more than four or five that day she sat on Mammy Sue's lap in the kitchen house, seeking soup and comfort. Mama and Papa were away, far away in England, and Priscilla wanted so much for them to come home. When they did that evening, however, after weeks abroad, Mama wasn't the same.

Later, Lettie, who was older and knew about such things, told Priscilla that Mama had given birth to a baby boy during those long weeks. But the son, that Papa had wanted so badly, had not lived, and there would be no others.

After that, Priscilla slipped into the kitchen house whenever she could and whenever Mammy Sue's lap was free. A few years later, Mammy Sue died and Mama continued to live. But it was as though they were both away. It was as though Mama had never come home from England.

*"Hi-ga!"*

"Priscilla jumped. "Yes! Yes, Straw Basket. *Hi-ga.* I'm eating."

She had often been accused of dawdling over her food, even when she was hungry, but Priscilla supposed it was best at the moment since it had been so long since she'd eaten. The bland soup set well, and, enjoying its flavor, she slowly, steadily emptied the bowl.

With her hunger alleviated Priscilla wished that the language lesson could continue, but Straw Basket had other tasks in addition to providing for her guest. No, not a guest, Priscilla reminded herself. *I-gi-do*—sister.

What an unexpected gift that was! She had wanted to adopt a sister once—an orphan girl who helped Mammy Sue in the kitchen house. Papa wasn't impressed, either, even though the little girl could read and write and recite the Lord's Prayer. Priscilla herself had taught her.

Priscilla and little Sally Ann were about the same age, and they had shared their deepest secrets—something that Lettie would never do. Mr. Davis expressed his disapproval of the relationship, but he didn't interfere until, in his mind, it had gone too far. That was the day Priscilla had proudly arrived at the dinner table with her hair painstakingly done up like her friend's. Every square inch of her head was covered with tiny braids in the finest picaninny style. Papa didn't say a word. But the next morning, he sold Sally Ann.

Priscilla sighed. She had no fear of being sold herself, although the thought had crossed her mind. Some Indians, she had heard, did keep slaves, but she had trusted the Lord to keep her from falling into their hands, and He had. Here, she would be a slave to no one; here she felt safe.

But was she? She wondered what it would mean to accept a place in a Cherokee family, a place in the Wolf clan. Straw Basket's invitation delighted her, but being her sister was one thing. It was quite another to be a daughter to some man and woman she had yet to meet! Perhaps they wouldn't welcome her so readily. And, if they did, they might place expectations on her, demands about what she could or could not do. They might even take it upon themselves to decide whom she should marry.

Bear Claw!

Priscilla shivered as she recalled the name. When Walkingstick had first mentioned the man, he had said that it would be good for Bear Claw to take her as his wife. At the time, those were only troublesome words, but since then, Walkingstick had acted upon them by bringing her to this village instead of to Chota. By now, others might have the same idea as the medicine man.

She wondered what ideas Garth Daniels had. Somehow she didn't think a marriage to Bear Claw was what he had in mind. He had mentioned sleepless nights on account of her, and that seemed unlikely if he expected her to become Bear Claw's bride. It could be that his activities as a trader included the bartering of people, but Priscilla didn't think so. Perhaps his interest in her welfare was simply because he was, in fact, a man of peace as he had proclaimed himself to be.

Love, joy, peace—the fruits of the Holy Spirit. But who would expect Garth Daniels to be a man of peace, a man of God? She supposed the Lord could use anyone, though. Even an arrogant man with boorish manners.

She wished she didn't find him so attractive, then wished even more that she knew when she would see him again. She needed his understanding of the language and culture, and she especially needed some advice on the matter of Bear Claw. She really should have done more to gain Garth as an ally, she supposed, but he had a way of antagonizing her that loosed her tongue. In the future, she would keep a watch over it, she vowed.

But now, the soup had appeased her hunger, making her drowsy once again. She snuggled as deeply into the mattress as the corn husks would allow, then closed her eyes.

"Soup 'n rest is best when you's a'mendin'," Mammy Sue used to say.

But Mammy Sue's cherished face wasn't the last Priscilla remembered as she drifted into sleep. Instead, she saw Garth Daniels' heavily lashed brown eyes, and she couldn't help but wonder if the owner was himself in need of a wife.

## CHAPTER 4

*Kaboom. kaboom.*

Priscilla peered through the doorway of the hut to watch the village women as they raised and dropped their heavy, wooden pounders in a low, echoing refrain. In front of every lodge stood a hollowed-out log that cradled the day's corn, and the pounders plunged against the oak, crushing and grinding the kernels into meal.

*Kaboom.*

For the last few days, Priscilla had risen little from her bedshelf, complying with the gestured orders of her adoptive parents to rest. But this morning she had awakened, refreshed and ready for adventure. She had bathed herself in the soothing herbal waters that Straw Basket had heated in an earthen pot, then she had donned a clean dress, cinching the loose garment with a leather sash around her slender waist.

How strange it felt to stand here wearing deerskin leggings instead of billowy skirts! But what surprised her more was seeing some of the women in European dress. Unkindly, she wondered what favors those few had granted Garth Daniels in return for the attractive but cumbersome gowns, then immediately, she chided herself for her assumptions. Just because he was a trader didn't mean that he dealt in women's fashions. Or in women.

He certainly had had no dealings with her, and for that, Priscilla was hard pressed to forgive. He had indicated that he would be back, but the better part of a week had passed, and still he hadn't come. She wouldn't care if she ever saw him again, she told herself, except that she had counted on his help in acquainting her with the people and their customs.

Actually, she hadn't done too badly without him. She and Straw Basket had continued with the system of pointing and identifying that they had devised, and through it she had learned the name of her adoptive mother—White Cloud. The father's name eluded her, and she couldn't bring herself to call him *e-do-da*, father, as Straw Basket did, but she had easily fallen into the habit of calling White Cloud *e-tsi*, mother.

Both adoptive parents had welcomed her with quiet solemnness, calling her daughter. But the Cherokee word, *a-que-tsi-a-ge-yu-tsa*, was far too long and the words for "Mourning Dove" even longer. Priscilla consistently failed to recognize it. Straw Basket solved the problem by teaching her parents Priscilla's Indian name in English, and the resulting Mourning Dove sounded quaint but, at least, recognizable.

The patterns of family life were somewhat recognizable too, the main difference being far less time for leisure. Although she had yet to venture beyond the entranceway of the hut, Priscilla had seen some of the children and men at play with stone-throws and stickball. At night, White Cloud sat by the fire, chanting softly as her fingers flew over some type of bead-work. Straw Basket, of course, used her spare time for the weaving that she loved, while her father joined his small family by the fire to whittle on what appeared to be a pipe bowl.

For the most part, however, daily life concerned the provision and maintenance of food, clothes, and shelter. Seldom did any members of the family eat together. Stopping, instead, they would scoop a chunk of bread or roasted meat or ladle up a bowl of vegetables or soup whenever hunger struck. By the time Priscilla breakfasted each morning her Indian father was long into the day's hunt for food.

She assumed, correctly, that other men in the village followed a similar routine of hunting for small game or fishing until their efforts were rewarded with catfish, bass, or brook trout. But if Bear Claw traveled among the men, Priscilla didn't know. Nor did she have any means of asking. Since she hadn't ventured out, she had yet to see a bear, or the claws of one, and until she did she had no way of pointing and identifying.

With her new language thus limited, she kept her eyes opened wider, taking in this foreign, yet familiar, culture. She was uncertain what her place in it would be, but it was fairly obvious now that her spiritual work could not interfere with the necessary physical chores required of every member of the village. She had to contribute *their* way before she could speak of *God's* way. She had to learn before she could teach.

*Kaboom. Kaboom. Kaboom.*

White Cloud moved her heavy pounder in unison

46

with the rest. Up, down, up, down, up. She stopped, her arms poised above her head, as Priscilla laid a hand on her shoulder.

"Let me help," Priscilla offered, pointing first to herself then to the pounder.

White Cloud shook her head.

"Please?"

The older woman laid down her large wooden mallet to feel the bit of muscle in Priscilla's thin arm. Then she shook her head again. But instead of continuing the job herself, White Cloud suddenly disappeared into the hut.

As soon as she was alone, Priscilla picked up the pounder and almost staggered under the unexpected weight. Still, she tried to lift the handle above her head as she had seen the other women do, but her aim went amiss. The mallet came down hard on the edge of the log, crushing not corn, but pride. More slowly she tried again, this time managing at least to hit the scooped-out center. But when she lifted the pounder, not a single kernel seemed to have suffered from her blow. Her third attempt succeeded in splitting a few kernels and in reminding her that she had unused muscles throughout her neck and shoulders. Then her fourth try had her wondering how anyone could keep this up for long!

Thankfully, Priscilla didn't have to. White Cloud returned with an empty vessel that she exchanged for the wooden mallet.

"*A-ma*," she said, and Priscilla nodded. Water. White Cloud wanted her to fill the clay pot with fresh water. A comparatively easy task, Priscilla thought.

Rather gaily, she set off in the direction of the stream toward which White Cloud had pointed. How good it felt to be outdoors in such beauty!

Around her, the village snuggled inconspicuously at the top of the hills below the mountains. Here, the smothering woods had been held at bay by fields of corn which, at the moment, bore only the stubby stalks remaining from the last harvest. As summer neared, the cycle of soil and seed, rain and harvest would begin anew, but now a far hillside blazed with a spring show of azaleas. Above that flaming slope hovered a smoky wisp of cloud, and beyond it, a blue, blue sky.

Priscilla inhaled deeply. Then, hugging the water pot to herself, she spun around slowly, her gray eyes sweeping the sky, the land, the village. This incredible place was her home. And there! That pole hut shingled in cedar was her house!

How small it looked from the outside. And yet, she saw, it was no different from the other huts scattered about the village, except that some had shakes of pine or hickory. One building, however, stood out from the rest. Built on a mound of earth, it had seven distinct sides which rose from the center of the village.

Priscilla stared at the strange structure, wondering at its purpose. The multi-fashioned sides must have some significance, she thought, and so must the building's placement at the heart of the humble town. A meeting place, perhaps. If so, then the layout was not unlike the towns she had always known. Why, it even had a plaza, a park, for ballgames and children's play!

She wondered why so few children were around. Back home, the plantation grew a prolific crop of black babies, like so much cabbage or cattle. Their status bothered Priscilla more after Sally Ann had gone because Papa forbade her then to have any future contact with the colored children. Since she couldn't teach them to read, the Bible would remain a mystery to them, forever belonging to the white folks.

That troubled her deeply until, on a spring day like this, she had opened up the windows all around, allowing in the breeze, and on it blew a chorus of voices, singing in the fields. She had heard them before, but the Negro Spirituals she heard that morning touched her spirit as church hymns and rituals never had, and then Priscilla knew. The slaves on the plantation were freer by far than she.

How free was Charles, she wondered now? She had no more desire to join him than she had to join the field hands. Yet she hoped he was glad to soar beyond that cloud-smoked curtain of sky. Somewhere, somehow, a heavenly life was his.

She couldn't imagine Charles' being happy here. He had hunted awkwardly when he had had to, and he had fished to no avail. Priscilla admired him for his efforts, for his willingness to try, but she couldn't see him regularly following those pursuits. He would have disliked the bland food, too, since it consisted always of corn in bread or mush or soup. To the Cherokee, she had learned, that corn, *se-lu,* meant life. But Charles had never liked corn.

*Ka-boom.*

The ever-present heartbeat sounded in her ears as Priscilla hurried toward the stream that ran alongside the village. Here, women of various ages and size had gathered to fetch water or to scrub clothes on the large, water-polished stones. Since a warm breeze played, most of the women had shed their deerskin dresses in favor of cloth ones like Priscilla wore, but one stood apart with petticoats and a long dress of dark red calico.

Priscilla tried not to stare. Even at a distance, she could see that the girl, perhaps sixteen, was a beauty. Her blue-black hair glistened in the sun as she moved, doe-like, among the rocks. Then suddenly the girl stilled, as though she had felt eyes upon her, and, regally, she straightened, returning Priscilla's stare.

All around, smiles vanished; chatter ceased as the women became aware of the intrusion. The idyllic scene which Priscilla had witnessed from an upper bank took on a somber air—as lifeless and unmoving as a painted canvas— with her on the outside. The only sound was the creaking of a locust branch; the only movement, the gentle swinging of a baby carrier that hung from that low branch.

Priscilla halted. Hesitantly, she smiled, scanning the upturned faces in hopes of finding some response, then, cautiously, she took a step or two.

"*I-gi-do!*" Straw Basket called the greeting first, and her face broke into its familiar smile. Without it, Priscilla had not recognized her, and she wondered at its delay.

"Sister!" she answered now. "*I-gi-do.*" And with that call, the still scene sprang to life again.

With the clay pot under her arm, Priscilla scrambled down the bank. Most of the women had returned to their work, but two or three moved toward her with shy curiosity to touch her creamy skin and long blond hair. Both were commonplace back home, but here it was entirely possible that these women had never seen a complexion as soft and pale as the ivory-colored dogwood blossoms that heralded the spring. Or touched hair as silken and bright as tassles on the early corn.

Priscilla stood quietly, allowing the gentle strokes.

Then laying aside her water pot to free her hands, she cupped the face of the woman nearest her, looking steadily into the short-lashed brown eyes. This she did with each of the women who hovered around. Touching their hair and skin as they had touched hers, she fingered a thick braid and brushed a cheek which was reddened with paint. Each movement brought a fresh eruption of giggles from the women.

"Hair like corn silk is worth much," a voice said, and immediately all laughter died.

Priscilla whirled to face the speaker—the girl in the calico dress. This close, she appeared even more beautiful than she had from afar, and yet less so. A hardness narrowed the large brown eyes, and a pout tucked the fullness from the girl's lips.

"You are Mourning Dove," the girl said before Priscilla could introduce herself. "I am Dancing Water, daughter of the chief, daughter of the Wolf clan."

"The Wolf clan! Then we're like sisters!" Priscilla exclaimed. "I am in the house of White Cloud and Straw Basket, also daughters of the Wolf clan."

"White Cloud and my mother are from the same womb, but you are sister to no one." The girl's eyes narrowed more. "Some of our people do not want a white woman here."

"I'm sorry to hear that," Priscilla said truthfully, "but I hope you'll accept me in time. I mean you no harm."

"So you say! My people have heard those words before from your real brothers and sisters," the girl said ungraciously. "Your people take the land. Now you come to take what is not yours."

"It's not like that," Priscilla insisted. "I have come to give, not take."

51

"My people need no gifts from you," Dancing Water retorted. "You have come like the others. You have come to take Bear Claw."

Nothing could have astonished Priscilla more. Feeling her mouth drop, she consciously closed it. And how was she to answer? Apparently this girl had set her heart on Bear Claw, and that suited Priscilla just fine. Unfortunately, however, the matter wasn't that simple. Since she had been unable to communicate with her new family, she didn't know what would be required of her if she chose to stay here. God himself had brought her, and He had be the one to tell her when it was time to leave.

Unwilling though she was, Priscilla had to face the fact that she might indeed have to marry Bear Claw. She measured her words carefully, praying God would provide even those.

"I can promise you this, Dancing Water, I will not take what is not mine."

The brown eyes were mere slits. "Nothing here is yours."

"Oh?" Priscilla couldn't help but smile. "Then tell me, Dancing Water. If you have such distaste for me and my people, why are you wearing a white woman's dress? Why are you speaking my language?"

The questions went unanswered. With a heave of her petticoats, the girl sprang lightly up the side of the bank, heading back to the village.

Priscilla had no intentions of following even before Straw Basket placed a restraining hand on her arm. Mere words couldn't alleviate the jealousy, the animosity that Dancing Water felt until Priscilla had had time to demonstrate to the girl and the other villagers that she had truly come in love and peace.

52

She patted Straw Basket's hand, still resting on her arm. Until now, it hadn't occurred to her that this young woman and her family had placed themselves in a precarious position in the community by inviting her to stay with them. Dancing Water had made it abundantly clear that some villagers would not be so welcoming. Worse, some might look with scorn or ill favor on Straw Basket's family.

Priscilla sighed. She had meant it when she had told Dancing Water that she wished her no harm. She wished harm to no one. And it troubled her now that she might inadvertently bring reproach to those very people who had been so kind. Something had to be done. But, at the moment, her only recourse was to be an obedient daughter to White Cloud, a helpful member of the family, a loyal sister.

Carefully stepping onto the natural bridge of large, round stones, Priscilla bent to dip the clay pot into the fresh-flowing stream. Cool, clear, life-giving water poured in, filling the container and reminding her that she herself was a vessel. God's vessels.

"Fill me too, Lord, and bring good out of my presence in this place."

Then, having already taken longer than intended, Priscilla called a goodbye to Straw Basket, who had returned to scrubbing her clothes on the rocks. She smiled, too, at the other women who chanced a friendly glance. Then, cradling the full vessel against her, she climbed the low bank, sloshing water down her dress front in the process.

Back home there had been servants—slaves—to haul water from the spring pump, and now Priscilla understood why those people possessed such strength, such sleek, well-developed muscles. A filled water pot was heavy! Heavier than the books she had carried from Papa's library. Heavier than the samplers she had patiently embroidered. Heavier than the silver teapot from which she had poured tea for her guests.

She wondered if she would make it back to the hut. Each step seemed to unloosen more the joining of arm to shoulder, and so she paced herself slowly, avoiding, she hoped, a wrenching jolt.

"Whatever things are pure, whatever things are lovely . . . if there be any praise, think on these things."

Snatches of Philippians 4:8 came back to comfort her, and Priscilla thanked God for the strengthening power of His word. She wished she knew more of it, wished she had memorized it more faithfully when she had the opportunity, for now her beautiful, leather-bound Bible lay on the floor of the river.

". . . whatever things are lovely . . ."

How lovely the mountains were today. How peaceful the village. How snug the humble huts. She had thought the dwellings were single rooms, but looking now, she could see that each had a tiny addition toward the back. How much there was yet to discover.

How much her arms hurt. Oh, it was no use. She set down the pot before she dropped it. Then she gave her shoulders a brisk rub.

". . . if there be any praise . . ."

She had to think about it.

"Praise God for water. For two arms. For . . . Garth!"

His very real and very timely appearance filled her with thankful relief. She knew she shouldn't let him carry the water pot since she had to become accustomed to hard work on her own. But just today. Just until she could build up her strength.

Approaching her in steady, long-legged strides, Garth swept her with his eyes.

"You're looking fit," he remarked casually, as if it were a chance comment on the weather. "I see White Cloud has you doing chores."

"I wanted to," she answered testily, as if he had just implied that she would much prefer to lounge about all day on satin pillows.

Coolly, Garth lifted his left brow. "Then why are you standing here?"

"I'm resting," Priscilla snapped.

"I see." His dark eyes skipped across her, laughing, but his lips held no trace of a smile. "Do you suppose you could rest while we talk?"

"I might be able to manage that," she said sarcastically.

"Good. I need to know why you're here, Mourning Dove."

Something in his tone, his bearing, made her feel that she'd been set before a black-robed, white-wigged judge, and her answer would determine her future for all time.

"I—I don't know," she said evasively.

"Priscilla! You must know. He shook his dark head impatiently. "Good grief, woman. You don't travel weeks beyond civilization only to arrive and not know why!"

"My actions are not quite as irresponsible as you deem them," she said with a lift of dimpled chin. "You must understand, sir, that I had no way of knowing exactly what to expect when we set out."

Garth's stern gaze softened. "Of course not. Surely you didn't expect to become a widow enroute."

"I wasn't thinking of Charles," she admitted. "I was thinking of the people themselves—the Principal People. Why do they call themselves that?"

"Because they are. To the Aniyv-wiya, all creatures are 'people.' Even the creatures of the forest. But there are Animal People and Principal People."

"That's just it!" Priscilla said. "I had expected the Cherokee, the Aniyv-wiya, to be little more than Animal People."

"And now?"

"I'm discovering that civilization has many forms."

Garth looked pleased with her answer. "But you still haven't told me why you're here."

"Oh." She was hoping he hadn't noticed. "I'm sorry, Garth, I—I doubt that you'd understand. If you were a Christian . . ."

"But I am."

It was her turn to be pleased. "You are? Oh, that's wonderful! That's . . ." *Odd*, she thought, for Garth's face had hardened.

Lettie is a Christian, she reminded herself, but Lettie had not understood. Perhaps Garth wouldn't either.

"Let me see if I have this straight," he said now. "You came here— a do-gooder—to convert the savages to a civilized worship of God. But you found more civilization than you bargained for, and now you question your original purpose."

The cynical statement was close enough to the truth to make Priscilla squirm uncomfortably under Garth's harsh stare. While she fumbled for words, he went on.

"You could, of course, stick it out until the heat of

56

summer. Your civil sensibilities will glazen then for reform, Mrs. Prescott—I guarantee it. You see, the women get quite warm, working hard in the cornfields, so they're apt to strip down to their waists. Ah," he said unmercifully, "your cheeks are pink already! But it's the winters, madam, when you'll really blush."

Garth stopped and pointed to the tiny addition to the huts that Priscilla had noticed earlier.

"Do you see the *osi*? That's a winter house. It's small, airtight, and protected by the earth mounded around it. During the months of heavy frost and snow, the family of this hut will move into that *osi*, which is aptly called a 'hot house.' It's stifling inside at times. And then the family members, male and female, will shed all clothes when they enter that warm chamber."

Priscilla's lips parted, but no words came.

"What will you do then, Mrs. Prescott? Will you shed your own modesty as well? Will you wrap yourself in cloth and melt, while White Cloud and her husband enjoy the freedom in which they were born? Or will you convert the family—indeed, the village— toward your chaste roast, which is so unlike heaven? Or perhaps you could convince the people to remain in their summer quarters, wearing layer upon layer of animal skins. But I must warn you. If you choose the latter, you'll have to be most persuasive, for the Principal People are not inclined, as the white man is, to demand more from the Animal People than is truly needed."

Garth inhaled deeply. "So, madam? What do you propose?"

Priscilla stood frozen, immobile, horrified by his revelation of this culture so alien to her own. She had

57

known, since the conversation with Dancing Water, that she could no longer burden White Cloud's family. Nor was she ready to leave when none of God's work had yet been accomplished.

Considering the picture that Garth had presented, Priscilla had no idea how she would cope. Regardless of his opinion of her, she had not set out to change the Cherokee culture. Instead, she had intended to adapt herself to it. But now! Naked in a hot house with Straw Basket and White Cloud and White Cloud's husband? God forbid.

"Mr. Daniels, I don't know what I'm going to do," Priscilla said frankly. "However, I have absolute confidence that the Lord who called me here will show me how I'm to minister. These people are His, and I mean to bring them Christ's name. But I haven't the faintest clue as to how I'll go about that. I'm sorry, but there's nothing more to tell."

"On the contrary, Mourning Dove, you've told me quite a lot. You've no intentions of going home yet, then?"

"That's correct."

"And I assume that you'll be most uncomfortable, come winter at least, if you have to live with White Cloud's family?"

"True. But, please understand, I've no wish to change their way of life, their means of survival."

"Understood," Garth said, and Priscilla thought she saw a glimmer of respect. "Then it seems to me that the only solution is for you to have a home of your own."

"Oh, I quite agree. But is that possible?"

"Not without insulting White Cloud and Straw Basket. Unless, of course, you should marry."

58

Priscilla sighed. "I was afraid of that, but it can't be helped. Until the Lord shows me that I'm to leave, I must stay, whatever the circumstances. Besides," she hesitated. "It seems that God has gone ahead of me in preparation."

Garth looked at her curiously. "What do you mean?"

"Bear Claw," Priscilla said, watching with some satisfaction at the startled expression on Garth's handsome face. It's my understanding that Walkingstick brought me to this particular village because of Bear Claw. I've yet to meet the man, but apparently he's lost a wife. Since I, too, am widowed, Walkingstick seemed to think my marrying Bear Claw would be a good thing."

"He's probably right," Garth grinned.

"Well, you needn't look so amused, Mr. Daniels!" Priscilla felt annoyed. This was her future, her married life she was talking about, and for her, there was little humor in it.

"Forgive me, Mourning Dove. It's just that you're handling this unusual situation rather stoically, as stoically, perhaps, as an Indian princess."

"I'll take that, sir, as a compliment, though I'm not unmoved by joy or grief, and neither, do I think, is the Cherokee."

"Very perceptive of you."

"At any rate, I haven't met Bear Claw. I don't even know if he speaks English," she said, almost to herself.

"Set your mind at rest, madam. He speaks your language rather well." Garth seemed to be enjoying her dilemma.

Priscilla shot him a look of annoyance. "Good.

59

Now, what I was about to say is that it seems odd that I was intended to become Bear Claw's wife, but instead I've become Straw Basket's sister.''

''Didn't you know? She was the same person.''

''What?''

''Bear Claw married Straw Basket's sister about three years ago.''

''Well, of course I didn't know. How could I? You didn't tell me,'' Priscilla said, exasperated. Then she wondered what else he hadn't told her.

''That's why you were taken to her family—to meet Bear Claw.'' Suddenly Garth laughed. ''I wonder if Walkingstick realized that he was causing a stir when he deposited you here?''

''I don't find that particularly amusing, Mr. Daniels. We're talking about my presence being a source of trouble, which is not what I had in mind.''

''Well, you'd better get used to trouble, madam, because Dancing Water may give you plenty of it.''

Priscilla frowned. ''I can handle her, I think. But what about her father? She said that he's the chief.''

''So he is. But Blazing Sun is a fair man, predisposed to peace. This is a peace town, you know.''

''I know, sir, only what you tell me.''

Garth smiled. ''There are around seventy towns in all. Some are designated as peace towns; some are war towns. From the city of Chota, the Principal Peace Chief presides in good times, and in turbulent times, the Principal War Chief has the final say over the entire Cherokee nation. But here, Blazing Sun is the local authority.''

Garth pointed to the seven-sided building that Priscilla had thought was a meeting place.

''That's the council house where people come

together for political, social, and religious matters. Each side of the building represents one of the seven clans—Paint, Blue, Deer, Bird, Wild Potato, Long Hair, and, of course, the Wolf clan. Blazing Sun presides over all of it, sitting behind the sacred fire.''

"Then, he's almost like a king.''

"Hardly,'' Garth scoffed. "Blazing Sun receives no birthrights, no inherited honors as do lords and ladies, knights and kings.''

"It's not always like that,'' Priscilla said defensively.

"Often enough,'' Garth insisted. "But Blazing Sun had to earn his honor before the people would elect him to his position.''

"Elect? You mean, the villagers themselves decided who their chief would be?''

Garth nodded. "Hard to believe, isn't it? The Principal War Chief and Principal Peace Chief are also elected. And not only that, but the women elect their most honored representative—the Beloved Woman of the Nation— who you may be interested to know, reigns in times of war or peace.''

"Oh, my.'' Priscilla was having difficulty taking in all that Garth was saying.

"Mark my words, Priscilla,'' he added now, "someday our people will tire of handed-down kings we've never seen or heard. Someday we'll be *civilized* enough to elect representation for our own colonies. And then, we just might have a government as workable as the Cherokees.''

"Perhaps, but I confess, at the moment I'm more concerned about representing myself to the chief.''

"I doubt you'll have to. If Bear Claw wants to marry you—and I'm certain he will—he'll have the task of confronting Blazing Sun." Garth seemed to be laughing at her again.

"Laugh if you will, sir, but if I were the chief, I don't think I'd like having my daughter cast aside a second time by the same man."

"The first time Dancing Water was too young. And now . . . we shall see," Garth said. "But don't forget, Mourning Dove, the Aniyv-wiya marry by mutual consent, not by force."

"I didn't forget." Priscilla stamped her foot. "You never told me." Her glare didn't silence his chuckles.

At one point, she would have been overjoyed to hear that no one could force her into marriage. Only this morning, in fact. But now, Priscilla had determined to marry Bear Claw as her best solution for remaining in the village. It didn't help, then, to know that Bear Claw could withhold his own consent.

She sighed heavily and looked at the flies collecting on the brim of the water jug. If she didn't return the filled container soon, the water would be unfit for consumption.

"I suppose we should be heading back," Priscilla said. "White Cloud will be waiting for the water."

"So she will," Garth agreed as he picked up the clay pot. "I just hope you won't find it too taxing. We still have much to talk about as we walk."

Then with a smirk and a slosh, he handed her the heavy vessel.

## CHAPTER 5

"YOU ARE NO GENTLEMAN!"

Garth laughed. "So I've been told."

"You might at least look ashamed of yourself."

"I might, but I won't." He fingered her hair, playfully at first then gently stroking it, much like the women had done by the stream. "I must say, Priscilla, that my eyes were hungry for a blonde."

"I'll thank you to keep your hands to yourself," she spat. "If my own weren't full—carrying this very, very heavy pot—I'd slap that grin from your face!"

"Don't ever try," he warned in a tone that showed he meant it. "The Aniyv-wiya don't take kindly to their people abusing one another."

"And what do you call this? I personally think it's abusive of you to walk along empty-handed while I'm still recuperating. And you're so big and strong and . . . ." She'd almost added "handsome," which had nothing to do with anything. It was just that ever since he had touched her hair, something within had quickened, some deep longing that she didn't understand and had tried to ignore.

"Don't take this personally, Mourning Dove," Garth said as she stumbled, wearily trudging up a slope. "You did say you wanted to be part of this village, these people, didn't you? Why, you're even willing to marry Bear Claw in order to stay. And he might be ugly and ancient, for all you know."

"Is he?" she asked, alarmed.

Garth chuckled. "Dancing Water doesn't think so."

"You're really no help," Priscilla said icily.

"Oh, but I am. I'm trying to point out that marrying Bear Claw is far more serious than carrying a water pot. Especially when the village women do all of the carrying and fetching. You'd better get used to it, Priscilla. The other women have. They know that their men must keep their hands free— to build, to hunt, to protect—even to kill if they have to."

She hadn't thought of that. What Garth said made sense, but that didn't stop her arms from hurting. She grimaced.

"Why don't you stop carrying that water pot like a white woman who's used to servants?" Garth said, sounding annoyed. "Here. Put it on your shoulder."

"I don't think I can," she admitted, and so he did it for her. Priscilla, however, withheld her thanks, feeling somewhat less than grateful.

"Tell me about Straw Basket's sister," she commanded rather sharply. She wanted to know as much as she could, and at the moment, she would be glad to have her mind elsewhere.

"Her name was Laughing Owl," Garth said in that soft voice, that special voice that made Priscilla think he had a heart.

"That's a lovely name. Was she beautiful?"

"Not like Dancing Water, but, yes, in her own way she was. Their mothers were—are—sisters, you know."

Priscilla nodded as well as she could with a clay pot on her shoulder. "Daughters of the Wolf clan. But what about Blazing Sun? Is he of that clan too?"

"Never. Members of the same clan are forbidden to marry," Garth said. "Blazing Sun is of the Paint People, but you might be interested to know that Nan-ye-hi, the Beloved Woman of the Nation, is a daughter of the Wolf."

"It seems I've been given a rather intriguing family," Priscilla said, delighted. "Oh, Garth, tell me about all of them!"

He laughed. "I will, but it'll take a long time."

Priscilla felt certain that the water jug had lightened with Garth's promise. Perhaps she was making too much of casual words, but her hopes leapt at his implication that they'd be seeing each other again. Then, just as quickly, her spirits sank. Bear Claw might not like the friendship that was forming between them.

Hesitantly, Priscilla broached the subject. "Garth, will Bear Claw object to our, uh, having contact with one another? Will he be jealous?"

"Hmmm." Garth stroked his clean-shaven chin thoughtfully, but the sparkle in his eyes belied his seriousness. "I should think, Mourning Dove, that that would depend on what you have in mind as contact."

"Oh, really, Garth. You are a dreadful man."

"Outrageous." Suddenly he stopped and whirled her around, catching the water pot before it drenched them both. "What do you want of me, Priscilla?"

"Want?" Her gaze shifted across his broad shoulders. "Why, information. Answers." She tried to keep her voice light.

Garth tipped her chin until he had captured her gray eyes. "And that's all?"

Her shallow breath came rapidly. "No," she admitted.

"What then? Friendship?"

She gave a feeble nod.

"Anything more?" His words pressed her as steadily as his hand.

"That's all there can be, Garth," she said and pulled away.

"I wouldn't be so sure, Mourning Dove," he said gently. "This is a different culture, a new world for you with fewer restraints. The man and women here have little time to win hearts. Or to hold them."

She wouldn't look at him again. Not with her chin quivering so.

"White Cloud has waited long enough for this water. Look, she's beckoning me to hurry."

Actually Priscilla thought her adoptive mother was waving flies away, but she had tarried long enough. Steadying the jug, she fled the spot where Garth still stood, but not fast enough to escape the laughter that he hurled against her aching back.

"Priscilla!" he called out. "Prissy! Bear Claw will be a most fortunate husband."

Oh, that man was outrageous. And yet, inside the dark interior of the hut, she couldn't stop herself from laying a cool hand against the dimpled chin he too had touched. The mere warmth of his fingers had sent ripples through her entire body—a sensation more foreign to her than the immediate surroundings of hearth and hut.

No, Bear Claw would not be a fortunate husband, she knew regretfully. Garth Daniels had seen to that. Although she had scarcely met the man, his magnetism drew her until she could not bear the thought of another man's touch. Not even Charles'.

Her alien emotions filled her with such shame, she sank onto the floor beside the fire and wept. She knew she was feeling sorry for herself, knew she wasn't trusting God's forgiveness or His love. But she cried anyway.

Maybe she had been mistaken all along. Maybe God had never called her here. Maybe she had only used the preacher's message as an excuse to get away.

And now that she was here, where could she possibly live? She would keep her eyes closed all winter if she had to. But she couldn't hurt Straw Basket or White Cloud by moving out, unmarried, when they'd been so kind. And yet she might hurt them more by staying. How terrible it would be if this family were ostracized by their own people because of her.

Oh, it was so unfair. But thinking about it only made her weep harder.

"Mourning Dove," White Cloud called softly, soothingly, as she padded across the dirt floor.

Priscilla sniffed and attempted a smile. "Oh, E-tsi, I wish we could talk; I wish you could understand what I'm saying. I just don't know what to do. Everytime I think I have an answer, I see that I haven't. And that dreadful man, Garth Daniels, confuses me even more.

"I don't want to hurt you by leaving," Priscilla went on. "Nor do I want to cause trouble for you by staying. I don't want to go home. But I don't want to marry a man who's not of my faith, a man I don't love, a man I've never met. Oh, E-tsi! What am I to do?"

The outpour of words lessened along with the sobs as White Cloud stood over Priscilla rubbing her sore shoulders and stroking her golden hair. The small, square hands brought comfort, just as Mammy Sue's larger, longer hands had done.

"Missy, no'un ever promised dat life wuz gonna be fair. But you has got de Lawd."

Remembering Mammy Sue's calming words, Priscilla smiled. Then she pressed White Cloud's rough hand against her cheek to let the older woman know it would be all right. Somehow, God would make clear what course was best. Until then, Priscilla knew the wisest choice was to trust God to work things out, to believe in the guidance He promised through His Holy Spirit.

With that decision consciously made, Priscilla laid aside her doubts, her fears, her confusion. The Lord had His work to do, and so did she—the most obvious being her need to master the chores required of a Cherokee woman.

Over the next few days, her language skills improved remarkably, but even without words, she learned quickly by watching White Cloud and Straw Basket. Step by step the women showed her the art of laying a fire, of cooking a meal, of carrying heavy burdens that weren't nearly so heavy, she discovered, when she knew what to do.

Using her head or shoulders or back kept at least one arm free for balance. Often she placed whatever needed carrying into a basket that hung down her back after being anchored with a wide strap across her forehead. This took some getting used to, especially since the weight thrust her forward as she walked.

Priscilla thanked God that she carried no living loads. The few women with children under a year or so were seldom seen without the forehead strap anchoring a stiff cradleboard across their backs. Or, if a woman didn't carry her own cradled infant, the burden fell to a grandmother or sister or aunt. Priscilla wouldn't want White Cloud or Straw Basket to be burdened thus, and she was still having enough difficulty taking care of herself!

Charles had been right to wait. No parent was ever truly prepared, but she was learning. When the time came, as she prayed it would, Priscilla hoped she would be ready enough.

Steadily, her strength increased, along with new knowledge and skills. As the weather continued to warm, she spent part of her daylight hours in the fields with other women and some of the men who had begun readying the soil for planting. Soon the Three Sisters would grow—corn, beans, squash. And, the Three Sisters would nurture the people of the village, sustaining them when the Animal People proved scarce.

With a freshly sharpened hoe, Priscilla upturned the dark brown earth, casting a wayward stone into a pile. Another downswing broke the clods into a finer texture just right for cradling seed.

When no one was looking, she knelt down to scoop up a handful of the dirt. Then she let it run between her fingers. She had seen Papa do so when he had stopped to admire his land, but Priscilla simply enjoyed the pleasure of being part of the earth's productivity. This land was God's.

The Principal People seemed to understand that, and Priscilla admired them for it. She had yet to learn by what name they called upon the Lord, but she had no doubt they did so, for chanting words and stances of uplifted hands showed a prayerful spirit evident in everyday life.

Once, she had tried to share with Straw Basket the good news of Jesus as Savior, but the experience had been frustrating to them both. Eventually, she had told herself, there would be no language barrier, and then Christ's name could take root as surely as the seed laid in a well-prepared field.

Meanwhile, Priscilla's actions spoke more eloquently than any language. With a jubilant spirit and a willingness to work, she had begun to gain a measure of acceptance—a nod here, a friendly gesture there. When someone had thrown a rock, hitting her on the shoulder, the people who witnessed the event shooed the boy away with a harsh scolding. Priscilla herself had intervened on the child's behalf, assuring the villagers with smiles and signs that she was unharmed. Yet it troubled her that Dancing Water had remained apart from the flurry with obvious malice marring that lovely face.

The girl had not spoken to her since the day of their meeting, and if anything, Dancing Water seemed more hostile. Priscilla couldn't understand such behavior. Nothing she said or did improved their relationship in the least, and she supposed that Dancing Water still considered her a threat. How ridiculous. Bear Claw had not approached her at all, much less asked her to marry him. If, however, he did, Priscilla knew what her answer must be.

She swung her hoe down hard. What a pity that the

people she had met thus far who spoke her language did not wish to be friends. Even Garth was avoiding her. She had seen him rarely in recent days, and then only from a distance. Arrogant man that he was, he probably expected her to race across the fields to greet him. Well, her heart did race. But, she had easily kept the rest of herself in check—probably because she'd spotted him coming out of Dancing Water's hut! Shortly thereafter, the girl herself had exited, wearing a conspicuously new, blue-gingham frock.

Dancing Water had on the same dress today, and Priscilla wondered if that meant Garth was still in camp. Probably. Seeking pleasure, consolation, passion? It was no business of hers what he and Dancing Water sought! Yet the more Priscilla thought about them, the faster she hoed.

She had to catch her breath when she saw Garth's familiar figure at last. What was it about that man that caused her own body to behave so unfamiliarly? Even her legs trembled beneath their leather strappings.

Unfortunately for Priscilla, Garth caught her staring across the length of the field. The sun flashed from his grin as he cocked his head and gave her a mock salute. Gladly, she could have wrung his neck when he hollered her name, calling attention to himself— and to her. Then, leaving her alone to face the resulting snickers, he slipped into Dancing Water's hut.

*How dare he.*

Priscilla threw down her hoe. Using more force than was necessary, she hurled the stones she had upturned, far beyond the perimeter of the field. Then she told Straw Basket she was going into the woods to gather kindling.

The cool forest air fanned the flush from her cheeks as she wandered down a deer path, carpeted with pine needles. Garth Daniels meant nothing to her, she told herself over and over again. Nothing, nothing, nothing.

Then why was he changing her into a person she didn't know?

"Look at me," she said to a chameleon, turning brown then green upon the forest floor. "We must be sisters."

The lizard darted away as Priscilla hurried up the path. Unconsciously, she headed toward her favorite retreat, a spot she had discovered when she first helped Straw Basket gather wood for the fire. She had gone back as often as she could since then until there was precious little kindling left.

Realizing this, Priscilla looked around until she found a stout limb that suited her purposes. Then she proceeded to clear the dead lower branches of a pine by giving them a sharp whack. That done, she advanced, club raised, on a promising-looking locust.

"Priscilla! Whatever are you doing?"

Club high, she whirled around to face Garth.

"You!"

"Would you put that weapon down before you hurt somebody!"

"I'm not finished," she insisted peevishly. "I've come to get kindling for the fire, and I'll not leave without it."

"Fine, but it can wait."

She eyed him suspiciously. "Why? What do you want?"

"To talk. That's all."

"How did you find me?"

He laughed. "Straw Basket pointed me in the general direction of your whereabouts, but the commotion you caused, getting a little firewood, could have alerted an army. Or a bear." Suddenly he sobered. "You shouldn't go into the woods alone, Mourning Dove."

"You needn't trouble yourself about my welfare, Mr. Daniels."

"Oh, but I must. Sit down Priscilla," he commanded, and she sat. "I've never really told you about Laughing Owl—what kind of person she was, how she died. I think it's time I did."

Primly, Priscilla sat on the rounded edge of a boulder, her fringe-covered knees tightly together, her hands folded expectantly in her lap. She didn't look at Garth, but gazed instead at the waterfall that had drawn her to this spot. The crystal beads of water rushed down a granite slope then settled peacefully into a moss-rimmed pool. Beside the mossy edge sprang the last of the spring violets, faded now from the warming sun.

"I want to know about Laughing Owl. Bear Claw too," Priscilla said. "And yet I—I don't."

"I'm not sure I understand," Garth admitted.

"Nor I!" She sighed. "Laughing Owl is my sister's sister. My mother's daughter. She's never been alive to me, Garth. If you make her so now, I'll only lose her. Or worse, I'll feel my new family's loss more deeply. I can't replace her, Garth."

"No one expects you to."

"Maybe not. White Cloud and Straw Basket have certainly welcomed me warmly as myself. But what about Bear Claw? What does he expect or need? The tremble in her voice surprised her. "It would make

73

matters so simple for me to marry. To have my own home, to . . . Oh, you know the reasons. But I've thought about it often since we talked, and I—I just can't go through with it."

Garth observed her coldly. "Why not, Priscilla? Does the idea of a Cherokee spouse seem loathsome to you?"

"Garth Daniels! You've twisted my meaning altogether," she said hotly. "Oh, don't you see? Bear Claw is only a name to me, no more real than Laughing Owl. But he's alive! He's a person with feelings and—and needs. How unfair it would be for me to marry him when I have no personal feelings for him."

"Perhaps you will," Garth said. "Don't close the door yet, Priscilla. I'm still convinced that it's the best solution for you. And for Bear Claw."

"You really think so? You really think I'd be good for him?"

Garth gave her a half-smile. "The best," he said.

"All right then, I'm ready to listen. Tell me about Laughing Owl "

"She was killed by a bear."

Priscilla's eyes snapped to his. "Are you saying that to frighten me?"

Garth acted as though he hadn't heard. "She wasn't even alone that day. In fact, she seldom was alone." He dropped onto a smooth boulder beside Priscilla and ran a hand through his thick hair. The fingers she thought, trembled ever so slightly.

"In a way, she was like you, Mourning Dove. As soon as Laughing Owl married, she left the village life she had known, choosing instead to be at her husband's side, no matter where he went." He paused. "Some Indian women do that, you know. Nan-ye-hi, the Beloved Woman, even followed her husband into battle."

"I didn't realize. So, Laughing Owl followed her husband everywhere."

Garth gave her a hint of a smile. "Not into battle, but, yes, she went hunting with him, fishing, traveling from place to place as there was need."

"What about children?"

"They had not yet been blessed with a child," he said sadly, "But when she died, a child was on the way." For a moment, Garth seemed lost in his own thoughts.

"Yes?" Priscilla prompted.

"She was gathering firewood— *quietly*, I might add—not far from the spot where her husband was building a lean-to of sorts. He was pounding a stake into the ground, when her scream alerted him. She had probably screamed before, but he hadn't heard. She didn't scream again."

"Oh, Garth."

"He was right there, Priscilla. So close. And yet, he might as well have been miles away."

"What did he do?"

"He ran. But even the wind wasn't fast enough to reach her in time. He flew at that bear with empty hands until his face and arm were half-torn apart, but he was too numb to care, to feel the pain. Finally, he found his knife. And he stabbed and stabbed and stabbed until the creature was long dead."

"That poor man," Priscilla said, weeping. "To lose both his wife and child in a single instant."

Garth looked at her in wonder. "Why, Mourning Dove! You're crying."

Well, of course, I'm crying." She sniffed. "Wouldn't anyone?"

"There are few tears shed by the Cherokee. Life is often hard here, Priscilla, and death is a real part of that life. It has to be accepted before a person can go on."

"I suppose. But it couldn't have been easy for Bear Claw to accept the loss of Laughing Owl and her unborn child—not if he believed he could have saved them by acting in time. Believe me, Garth. I know."

"Charles?"

She nodded. "He was safe. He had latched onto a log and was moving downstream rapidly, away from me. I think I screamed; I don't remember. But I'll never forget his face when he turned and saw me. It was as though, for a moment, he had forgotten I was there. He looked startled. And then, treading water, he hurled the log upstream with a single hand. I remember thinking what strength that took, and I wondered how he had done it. It wasn't a big log, but Charles was of slender build. That effort must have cost him his last breath." Her voice broke into sobs.

Garth held Priscilla's hands in his own, saying nothing. When at last she had composed herself, she went on. "I had taught myself to swim, but my skirts weighted me down. I reached the log as quickly as I could, and kicking and paddling, I maneuvered it downstream. Somehow I pulled Charles onto it. Somehow we reached the shore. I collapsed, Garth. I couldn't move—even though Charles needed me."

"You did what you could." Garth put his arm around her until she stopped shivering.

"He was dead," she said simply, "with that same startled look forever on his face."

"Then that proves it. He didn't live long enough to reach the shore," Garth insisted quietly. "He made the choice, Priscilla, when he let go of that log. So you mustn't blame yourself or him. He wanted you alive. And so do I."

Sniffing, she shook her head. "I heard him groan. I know I did."

"Little Dove, you heard only yourself, not Charles."

The guilt unloosed its hold as Garth's words and arms enveloped her. Priscilla rested against his shoulder, listening to the waterfall— turbulent, yet peaceful, like her own heart.

"Did it occur to you, Mourning Dove, that God is bringing good out of two tragedies."

"Yes, but I don't see it yet," she admitted.

"In time you will."

His warm breath settled on her hair as she leaned, contented, against him. This was the way it should be, she thought, safe, secure, in someone's arms.

No, not someone's. Garth's.

Reluctantly, she pulled away. "I wish I'd known Laughing Owl," she said, feeling a need to break the too comfortable silence.

"You would have liked her. She was as kind as White Cloud, as attentive as Straw Basket, as spirited as Dancing Water. So bright, so alert, so alive." His voice softened until Priscilla had to strain to catch his words. "I've seldom met a woman like Laughing Owl."

"Why, Garth! You sound as though you were in love with her," Priscilla blurted out.

Immediately, she regretted her words as the color washed from his face.

"I was."

Ridiculous tears stung Priscilla's eyes as she stood abruptly. She had suspected all along that Garth enjoyed the company of the village women, Dancing Water among others. But she had never thought he would desire another man's wife.

"I—I'm sorry. I didn't know." She bit her lip. "I mean, Laughing Owl was . . . was married to someone else, and . . ." Her eyes suddenly widened. "Garth! She was, wasn't she?"

He shook his head. "No, Mourning Dove. Laughing Owl was married only to me." Lightly he touched the scar on his face, a jagged reminder of his futile attempt to save his wife and child. "I am Bear Claw."

## CHAPTER 6

PRISCILLA FLEW AT HIM, pounding, kicking, sobbing. Garth allowed the blows until she sank into his arms, exhausted. Then he scooped her onto his lap, rocking her like a child until she had thoroughly quieted.

Tenderly his lips brushed her forehead, and a gentle hand stroked her hair.

"Marry me, Mourning Dove."

His tightened hold prevented her from lashing out again. She struggled to get up.

"Let go of me, Garth Daniels!"

"Not until you say you'll marry me."

Futiley, she pushed at his arms, his hands. "I told you I wouldn't marry Bear Claw!"

"Ah!" He gave her a squeeze. "Your reason, I recall, was that you had no personal feeling for the man. Surely you can't deny plenty of feelings for *me*—even if, at the moment, they are angry ones."

"Quite." Deliberately, she stilled herself, back erect, chin lifted, as though she were a doll with no

79

emotions whatsoever. Garth Daniels would not toy with her. She would not have it. No matter how long it took, she would sit here, she resolved—rigid, unmoving—until he wiped that smug grin from his face.

She couldn't stop, however, the heat that flushed her throat and crept slowly up her face. Nor could she stop her quickening heartbeat. A single finger touched the nape of her neck then circled her ear until it paused, maddeningly, on a telltale pulse. She held her breath.

"Don't try to fool me, Prissy. You're not indifferent to me, even though you may wish it."

She said nothing, but glared at him instead from the corner of one eye. The smug grin was gone, she noticed with satisfaction, but another look had taken its place. She turned to him more fully, and his lips came down, hard, on hers. His waiting hand captured the back of her head, and his other arm locked around her waist, gripping her in a smothering embrace.

She thought she had suffocated, but her quick breaths assured her she had not. What was she doing? Murmuring his name! What was he doing? Kissing her lips, her cheek, the tip of her nose! And how did her arms get there, around his neck? Abruptly, she pulled away.

"Don't get prissy on me now, Mourning Dove," Garth chided. Playfully, his lips tugged at her ear lobe.

Priscilla felt herself redden. One thing was certain. Garth Daniels' view of marriage would not be the same one held by Charles.

"You should know I'm not as *experienced* as you," she said hotly.

He chuckled softly. "And what, may I ask, does that mean?"

Priscilla glowered at him from beneath her long lashes. "I'm referring to the disproportionate number of European dresses floating around this village. They bear witness, I believe, to your—your escapades." She hated her priggishness, but continued snippishly. "Dancing Waters' blue gingham was especially fashionable."

To her surprise, Garth laughed outright. "Silly Priscilla, I believe you're jealous!"

He caught her hand before it reached his face, imprisoning it easily in a bone-crushing grip. "I warned you before—you'll not slap me. Do you understand?"

"I understand that you provoke me, Garth Daniels," she shouted. Yet despite her fiery words, her arm, her hand, went limp. Quickly she shut her eyes, barricading tears.

Garth wiped away the trickle that followed the curve of her cheek. "I'm sorry if I hurt you." His moistened finger slid to her lower lip, tracing it and making it tremble all the more. "Look at me," he commanded. Then, "Please."

She opened watery eyes.

"I'm a trader, Priscilla," he patiently explained. "My business is trading the items one would normally purchase in a mercantile—tools, iron pots, blankets, even dresses if a woman so desires." He slipped an arm around her. "Personally, I think the native clothing is more practical for the life encountered here. But regardless of my preferences, I trade what the people want for what they have. In return, I receive baskets, beadwork, furs and sometimes favors. But not, my dear, those favors that you suggest."

She wanted to believe him, but her own eyes made that impossible. "I saw you, Garth. Going into Dancing Waters' hut on more than one occasion. Each time she came out freshly gowned."

"Priscilla, as long as Dancing Water wants new dresses, I'll bring new dresses. But I wasn't visiting her; I was talking with Blazing Sun. I thought you understood that the good will of the village chief needs cultivating if you're to stay here."

"You mean you've been speaking to him on my behalf?"

Garth nodded. "Ever since your arrival."

"But I thought this was a peace town."

"It is. Much like the cities of refuge established by the Hebrews in Old Testament days." He cocked his head. "What? Are you astonished that I'm familiar with the Bible? Rest assured, my dear, my mother taught me well."

Garth shifted her scant weight on his lap. "At any rate," he went on, "you're safe enough in this place, but that doesn't guarantee the regards of those around."

"I'm aware of that," she snapped, "and I'm capable of earning that esteem."

"Are you?" He smiled at her as though she were a child. "That's splendid. Then I won't have to worry about you while I'm away."

"Away!" Priscilla exclaimed. "But, I thought . . . ." No, she couldn't tell him that she had hoped to see more of him if they married, not less.

"I seldom remain long in any camp, though you sorely tempt me to stay here forever, Mourning

82

Dove.'' His lips brushed the back of her neck. ''Come with me.''

''You know I can't,'' she said regretfully. ''My work is here. The only reason I'm considering marriage at all is so I can remain here in peace and privacy.''

Somehow that didn't come out exactly the way she had intended, Priscilla thought. She meant to suggest that she was too soon widowed to remarry just yet. Garth of course, would have little patience with such proprieties, but she doubted the truth would make him as angry as he appeared to be now.

''Don't use me, Priscilla.''

''Don't expect me to be Laughing Owl.''

''I m not.''

''Well, I'm not using you either.''

He raised a dark brow. ''How can I be sure?''

She had merely planned to kiss him lightly, to show him her affection, her caring for him as a person. But the kiss deepened until nothing existed but his warm breath upon her cheek, his lips upon hers. His hands caressed her, his arms pressed her tightly against him until she, a willing captive, thought her head, her heart would burst. Then, without warning, he thrust her away from him. She could only stare, dumbfounded.

''You'd do anything to stay here, wouldn't you?'' As he spoke, Garth rose, almost dumping her on the forest floor.

''That's not true,'' she said in a voice as shaky as her knees. ''I wouldn't have kissed you if I hadn't wanted to.''

''Wanted to what?'' he asked, disgusted. ''Wanted to stay here? Wanted to show me you would make it worth my while? Then you can save those innocent tears, madam. You have proven your point exceedingly well.''

''But I didn't . . . .''

Garth's hand tore through his hair. ''Let's not argue. You have your reasons for wanting to marry me; I have mine. We'll marry before the week is out. And may God help us both.''

Stunned, Priscilla stood gaping after him until he was long out of sight. Then she sank into a heap, giving into the tears that had annoyed Garth so.

What had she done wrong? she wondered. She had only wished to demonstrate her caring, but instead he had practically accused her of harlotry. Well? Was she guilty? Priscilla wasn't sure.

She'd married Charles for the noblest of reasons: so that they, together, could commit themselves to God. Neither of them, however, had given much thought to their commitment to one another, Priscilla realized now. And, according to Garth's jaded view, she was about to do the same thing again.

No, he hadn't been quite so generous. Instantly he had assumed that she was enticing him in order to get her own way. The audacity of that man! Priscilla didn't know why she cared, but she did. In fact, his vexation arose because she cared more than she had dreamed possible.

''Why, Priscilla Prescott,'' she exclaimed to herself. ''You're falling in love with that barbarous man.''

Struck by this absurdity, she gave an ironic laugh. Lettie would have plenty to say if she were here, and Priscilla thanked God that she was spared, at least, that upbraiding. It was enough to recriminate against

the charges made by one's own self. Savagery—
that's what it was, wasn't it? Her savagely passionate
response to Garth had shocked her far more than it
did him, and she blushed again, just thinking about it.

He would never believe her admission of love.
Never. Unless . . . unless she proved her caring by
leaving the village, by going with him as Laughing
Owl had done.

At first Priscilla spurned the idea. She wasn't
Laughing Owl, and she had no wish to emulate her.
However, another consideration occurred that she
could not cast lightly aside: God had called her to this
territory, but not necessarily to this particular spot.
By traveling with Garth, she would come in contact
with many people in many areas. And, she would
have the advantage of remaining at her husband's
side.

The more she thought about it, the better she liked
the idea. With a lightened heart, she gathered the
firewood she had broken off earlier, laying it neatly
into a pile. As she worked, she hummed, her mind
singing lyrically of Garth.

"Mourning Dove."

Priscilla turned with a start. "Straw Basket! I didn't
hear you coming." She wouldn't have heard anything,
she realized.

"Bear Claw send. He say no good in wood alone."

"He did?" Priscilla was amazed. Even though
Garth had stormed off, he had still given thought to
her safety. She smiled. "Did he tell you we're soon to
be wed?"

Straw Basket shrugged, not comprehending.

"Marry," Priscilla said slowly. She held up one
hand, "Bear Claw." She held up her other hand,

"Mourning Dove." Then, bringing the two together with fingers intertwining, she said, "Marry."

Straw Basket beamed. "Marry. Good."

"Oh, I hope so," Priscilla laughed. "I sincerely hope so." She gave Straw Basket a hug, then gathered up her kindling.

When she had drunk in a last look of the waterfall, Priscilla headed back to the village with Straw Basket close behind. Indeed, her sister shadowed her constantly over the next few days until Priscilla began to wonder just what Garth had said. She would have asked him herself, but, once again, he made himself scarce.

She supposed Garth thought there was nothing more to discuss, although he could, at least, tell her what day they would be married! He had said before the week was out, but in this place, it was difficult to distinguish one day from the next.

Priscilla did have the assurance, however, that the wedding would occur as planned. For one thing, White Cloud spent every spare moment sewing beads on a soft white leather dress, fringed at the knees, which Priscilla presumed would be hers for the wedding. White Cloud had helped her try on the dress, satisfied then that it was a well-shaped fit. The thin leather molded itself nicely, smooth and supple against her own skin.

But it was Dancing Water's dress that convinced her that Garth's proposal had not been a dream. The girl wore new pink-sprigged cotton that Priscilla couldn't help admiring. Her husband-to-be, it seemed, had rather good taste in women's fashions, despite his disclamor that the native costume was best. But if he thought he could trade gowns for the girl's good will, Priscilla knew he was sadly mistaken.

Dancing Water's hostility had become almost tangible since the wedding news had spread throughout the village. Whenever possible, she directed harsh words or looks toward her rival until Priscilla wondered about her own safety. Straw Basket's constant presence reassured her, as Garth had obviously intended, but even a beloved sister was a poor substitute for Bear Claw's protective arm.

If only she could see him. A mere glimpse now and then wasn't enough. She longed to be with him, talk to him, let him know that she intended to go with him, wherever that might lead. But, when no opportunity presented itself, Priscilla decided to seek him herself.

The few times she had caught sight of him since their encounter in the forest, he had been coming from a section behind the osi, which she had yet to explore. Of late, other men had been in that area, a fact in itself that Priscilla found curious, especially when White Cloud's husband appeared among them. What, she wondered, was going on?

As soon as she could get away, undetected, Priscilla skirted around the hut and osi, away from the fields, the stream, and the favorite spot she had found in the woods. On the edge of the village, this parcel of land looked as though it had once been separated from the forest by a solid wall of log fence. Time had worn down the fortification, leaving only a partial barrier, but the semi-protected area was not forgotten. Men swarmed about on the freshly cleared land, building some kind of structure, and, as she had expected, Garth was among them.

Nearing the spot, Priscilla had an impression of a forest of legs, with only Garth's fully clothed. She wondered if she would ever get used to the breechclout that most of the men wore—the leather oblong that hung, front and back, from a strap tied about the waist. In warm weather, the scanty garment was certainly practical but, by her standards, immodest. She knew she was blushing even before Garth spied her.

Their eyes locked as he came toward her. "Did you want me, Priscilla?"

She glanced off toward the new building, rising rapidly before her. "What are you helping the men build?" she asked.

Garth snorted. "I'm not helping them build anything. They're helping me. That's your house, Priscilla." He waved an impatient hand. "Did you think it would just magically appear?"

"I—I hadn't thought . . . ."

"Obviously," he said. "Well, what is it you want? I can't leave the men at work while I stand about chatting."

"Tell them to stop."

"What?"

"You heard me. They mustn't build a hut no one will occupy." This was not the romantic scene she had envisioned, but now she had little choice but to blurt the truth. "I've decided not to stay in the village, Garth. I—I want to go with you."

He stared at her with aversion. "Oh no you're not. I wondered how long it would take for Dancing Water to get under your skin, but I must say I'm disappointed, Priscilla. I thought you would manage the girl somehow."

Priscilla couldn't believe this was happening. "I did. I can. I mean . . . ." She wrung her hands. How could she possibly avow her undying love when her intended spouse was standing, hands on hips, shooting daggered looks at her.

"Never mind," she said. "Forget I came." Hastily, she retreated, her back hiding a rush of tears.

"Priscilla!" he called out, but she broke into a run.

Thankfully, White Cloud and Straw Basket were doing chores elsewhere when Priscilla reached the sanctity of their hut. Breathless, she slipped inside the dark interior, then stood there trembling. Garth must certainly think her a simpleton now!

How different things might have been if she had responded positively when he had first asked her to come with him. But, no, she couldn't have done so then—not until she knew her own mind, her own heart. Now it was too late, the hut too close to completion to say she would not be needing it. But she *had* said. She had told Garth, and he had immediately assumed she had meant to escape Dancing Water's lashing tongue.

Admittedly, the girl presented problems that could intensify after the wedding. Garth would be gone, and Priscilla would no longer have the security of White Cloud's family. As daughter of the chief, Dancing Water could easily stir up resentments. Yet despite the hateful possibilities, Priscilla trusted God to protect and guide her. What she felt now was sheer disappointment. She and Garth would not be together after all.

He came to her at dusk, before the sky had purpled, drawing her into the blackening shadows behind the osi. Atop a small ridge, their hut stood silhouetted against the evening light. Garth pointed to it, his long finger curving with the arc of the winter house.

"We'll finish the osi tomorrow, Priscilla, and after

89

that . . . ." He stopped, his voice brittle. "Have you changed your mind?"

"Nothing's changed, Garth." *Only my awareness,* she added to herself.

She shivered, and he placed an arm around her. Priscilla stiffened beneath his touch, every sense alerted. She could tell he was still angry with her, the muscles of his arm tensed across her back. What would it be like after they married if neither of them let go of wariness, if neither yielded?

Deliberately, she rested her head against his chest as they stood gazing at the hut. Their hut. Slowly, she relaxed against him, breathing a contented sigh.

Garth froze. "What are you thinking about? Charles?"

She flung herself away from him. "Why do you ask that?" Her eyes narrowed. "Unless you were thinking about Laughing Owl."

He winced. "No. I was wondering why you had, I don't know, softened."

Priscilla lifted her dimpled chin in a vain attempt to stop its quiver. "Apparently I used poor judgment," she snapped.

In the gathering dark, she caught a glimmer of his smile. "Any mistake, my dear, was mine."

Tenderly, then, his arms went round her trembling shoulders, her tiny waist, and he held her to him, her head resting just beneath his strong chin. His warm breath stirred her silken hair, and his pounding heart awakened her own.

When his lips discovered hers, Priscilla tipped back her head eagerly, giving herself up to his kiss. She had had none like this delicate flutter, this winged search that sent her, a fledging, into flight.

Beneath Garth's moonlit eyes, she felt herself grow suddenly shy. "Tell me about the wedding ceremony," she asked, scarcely recognizing her own voice.

"You'll be there, and I'll be there," he teased, "as will the entire village."

"Everyone?"

"Of course. The Aniyv-wiya work hard, Little Dove, but that doesn't mean they don't like to play. Our wedding will provide a suitable excuse."

She laughed. "I didn't realize we were such an attraction."

A feathery finger traced her lips. "Ah, Little Dove, this is the attraction." He kissed her again, lightly.

"Who who will perform the ceremony?" she asked a moment later.

His hands dropped to hers, giving them a reassuring squeeze.

"*We* will," he answered, matter-of-factly.

Shocked, Priscilla's gray eyes flew to his. "But—I—we . . ."

Garth let go of her hands, and his arms folded across his chest.

"Prissy, were you expecting the woods to yield a preacher or a priest?" he taunted.

"No. It's just that . . . ."

"That what?"

She didn't know. She hadn't thought about it until now. Oh, of course, she knew there would be no church organ, no satin gown, no waiting pews. But to marry without a proper clergyman . . .

"Is it possible to have a civil ceremony?" she asked, embarrassed.

"As opposed to an 'uncivil' one," he remarked

91

coldly. His eyes swept her pityingly. "Well, madam, would a judge do?"

"I suppose so," she said, hesitantly. Then with vigor. "Yes! A judge would be fine," she added, bravely hoping that Garth had someone in mind.

"Splendid," he said, although his tone didn't correspond. "We'll marry the day after tomorrow then."

"And the judge?" she pressed him. "He'll be here then?"

"Naturally, I'll be here," Garth drawled.

"You?"

"I wasn't always a trader, Priscilla. For years, I studied law—even entered my father's firm." He looked away. I had a stroke of good fortune with other people's ill fortune," he said bitterly. "The results brought my name before a clamorous populace who wanted me for a judge. Those in authority listened, and the appointment came with amazing speed."

"Why, Garth, I'm impressed."

"Don't be. This life suits me better, Priscilla. I just pray it suits you."

## CHAPTER 7

WITH NERVES ATINGLE. Priscilla slipped the leather dress over her blond braids. Today she would become Priscilla Daniels. Mrs. Garth Daniels. She repeated her new name over and over, savoring the sound. Judge and Mrs. Daniels, she thought, then waved a hand. No, he wouldn't like that.

Her pride in him seemed to annoy Garth, who had refused to discuss his background further.

"Get it through your head, Prissy. The person you see here is the man you're marrying," he had said. At the time, his abruptness had wounded her because of the ensuing chill, the remoteness she had felt return to their relationship. But today was different. Today they were to wed.

Somehow they had agreed that the traditional ceremony of the Aniyv-wiya would be followed by their own private vows spoken in the intimacy of their newly finished hut. Lettie would have a conniption if she knew, but Priscilla decided she had to pursue her own course.

Close at hand, however, her adoptive sister beamed. Straw Basket and White Cloud hovered over her, clearly expressing their approval and contributing in their own way. The beaded handwork sparkled on the leather dress, and now both women tediously threaded more strands of beads through Priscilla's hair.

"Pretty," Straw Basket pronounced when they had finished.

"*Wa-do, E-tsi, I-gi-do.*" Priscilla twirled around. "Oh, I'm so nervous." At their questioning brows, Priscilla outspread her trembling hands. "See?"

White Cloud clasped the shaking fingers in her own warm ones, rubbing them in a calming, circular motion.

Straw Basket looked on with a grin. "Bear Claw good man," she said. "Mourning Dove good sister, good wife."

Priscilla's eyes misted. "I hope so." If love were enough, it'd be true.

But what about Garth? Would he come to love her, too, in time? She knew he found her attractive, perhaps even desirable. But would he accept and appreciate her as he had Laughing Owl? A shadow crossed Priscilla's face, and in that fleeting moment, she felt like running. How would she explain her unusual situation? He didn't strike her as the sort of man who could comprehend a celibate marriage, regardless of the noble reasons.

*What have I gotten myself into?* she wondered with gnawing apprehension. She had heard that some unchaste girls feigned innocence on their wedding night. Was it possible to pretend the opposite? If Garth taunted her, Priscilla thought she would die of misery.

94

No time to back out now. White Cloud solemnly laid a sheath of corn across Priscilla's quaking arms then draped a fresh blanket across her shoulder. The older woman nodded as Priscilla stepped hesitantly to the door.

Once outside, the small party progressed towards the large dome-shaped council house that stood in the center of the town. As she walked steadily toward it, Priscilla kept her eyes, trancelike, on the dome while all that was around her took on an ethereal quality. It was as though she walked through a painting of colored chalk, smudged by some giant hand that excluded the council house, leaving it alone sharply delineated. Smoky clouds cloaked the mountains. A fog-like veil muted the thatched huts scattered around and a smeary mist curtained the plaza where villagers had danced for her wedding and would dance again. And even the drums, the chants, the hissing shakers were slowly muted into silence.

This wasn't real. But there was Garth, his eyes softened by the dream, smiling handsomely as she floated toward him in the center of the town house. She had been told that the whole village would be there, but at that moment, there were only the two of them, caught in this alluring spell.

In a low voice for her alone, Garth was telling her how beautiful she looked. Then he was quietly instructing her on the trade of her corn for the leg of venison he held. The exchange, he explained, symbolized their obligation and their promise to provide for one another. Within the blissful cloud, his gift, her gift, exchanged hands.

And then, Garth slipped a blanket from his arm, and she, a shimmering mirror, followed his every move.

95

His fingers, her fingers, his blanket, her blanket touched, wrapped, knotted into one—a single unit, two halves made whole.

"This symbolizes our sharing the same bed," Garth said quietly.

The surrounding rainbow burst. Priscilla blinked. She looked around. Dozens and dozens of olive faces, berry faces looked back. Men, women, children sat, according to social status, on the bleacher seats circling the large room. Everyone stared, somber. Everyone had watched. Everyone had come to see the blankets tied.

"That's it," Garth said cheerfully.

"That's it?"

He nodded. "We're married, Mourning Dove."

"Married?"

And then, mortified beyond endurance, she fainted.

When her gray eyes fluttered open, the first thing Priscilla saw was stars coming through a hole. She closed her eyes quickly and opened them again, but the view didn't alter. She shifted, slowly becoming aware of thick blankets between her and a dirt floor.

Outside, the sounds of laughter, songs, and stomping feet filled the air, but inside all was quiet except an occasional shuffle, muted and low. Beneath the starry hole, someone had lit a fire that blazed now cosily, and silhouetted against the flame, a crouching man moved about.

"Garth?"

The darkened figure paused, then crept toward her. His hand settled kindly on her forehead, smoothing away the wisps of hair and stroking either temple.

"You're all right, Little Dove, though you've missed the celebrating on our behalf."

"Oh, Garth. I feel so ashamed." She rolled away, covering her face with her hands.

"What happened, Priscilla?"

"I don't know." She scooted onto an elbow and squinted up at him as her eyes adjusted to the dark. "It was like everything was a dream, all hazy and unreal. And then, suddenly, it wasn't."

Glad for the shadows to hide her flaming cheeks, she remembered that awful moment when an entire village witnessed her and Garth's intentions of physical union. No such thought had entered her mind when she had wed Charles, although she had had a vague notion of that being part of their married life, a small part of their glorious plans. Now, to have a whole town witness such intimate thoughts made her feel naked before them.

"Priscilla, when is the last time you've had something to eat?"

"Oh." She hadn't thought of food for at least a day.

When she told him so, he looked grim. "No wonder you fainted. Is this the way you're going to take care of yourself while I'm away?"

She didn't respond, and he gave an impatient snort. Then he rose, returning to the fire from which, she noticed now, good smells wafted.

"Eat this," he commanded, shoving a wooden bowl into her hands.

Steadily she ate, commenting on the discovery of yet another of his talents. The thick soup settled her stomach, but, more, it settled her anxiety. If Garth thought nerves and hunger had brought on a fainting spell, he wouldn't be inclined to probe further, she hoped.

When she had scraped up the last bite of vegetables

and drop of broth, Garth replaced the empty bowl with a cup of soothing herbal tea. Priscilla sipped it appreciatively.

"Did you know," she teased, "that if we only married by tribal law and custom, your name would have to be Garth Davis?"

"Don't let it go to your head." Playfully, he poked her, causing her tea to slosh.

"Now look what you've done," she scolded.

In mock exasperation, Garth slapped his forehead. "Spare me! A nagging wife already!"

She giggled. Then catching the odd look in his eye, Priscilla sobered.

"Having doubts?" he asked.

"Some," she admitted, not looking at him as she dabbed at the tea spill.

"I see." He sounded disappointed.

She looked up quickly. "Not about you, Garth. About me."

"You're stronger than you think, I expect." His voice held a note of relief. "I'm sorry I'll have to be away much of the time, but it can't be helped."

"I understand, Garth. You've no need to apologize."

"I'm not. I'm simply expressing my," he hesitated, "remorse." He tipped her face up to catch the firelight. "Don't fret, Priscilla. Blazing Sun is your ally—for now."

"What do you mean?"

"Times are changing. Our people are crowding in on the Aniyv-wiya, and a clash will eventually disturb even the peace towns. But I'll be out there. I'll know when a conflict erupts."

"Oh, Garth!" Without thinking, she squeezed his

98

hands. "Promise me you'll not place yourself in any danger."

"I wasn't planning on it," he answered dryly. "I'm well aware, Priscilla, that you're marrying me for protection, and I don't intend to let you down." Ignoring her small protest, he went on. "I can make no guarantees, of course, but I want to be able to come home to you and a passel of blond children."

Shyly, Priscilla lowered her lashes. "I make no guarantees either."

"Then how about dark brown hair and dove-gray eyes?" Garth teased.

Priscilla chewed her lower lip as he raised her face again to the flickering light. Was her chin trembling? Or was it his hand?

"No more mourning about the past, Little Dove?" His soft voice queried. "No more fretting about the future?" Then, satisfied by her small nod of assent he declared, "I want you, Priscilla."

"Enough to marry me," she answered with a trace of bitterness.

Garth sighed, not denying it, and she supposed she should be grateful that he found her so attractive. Perhaps in time he would come to love her as she did him, but they had so little time. She couldn't help but regret his lack of caring for her as a person, a companion, a wife. How much better it would be if they were partners of the mind and of the spirit as well as of the flesh.

"Are you ready to get on with our *civil* ceremony," he asked.

She took a deep breath and nodded, thinking that the tying of the blankets was the only part of any ceremony that interested Garth. His next words, then, surprised her.

"I've been thinking what might be special to you, Priscilla, and I'm ashamed to admit that it didn't occur to me until then that you've probably missed having a Bible. I assume yours was lost in the river."

"Yes."

"Well, consider this one yours," he offered. "But before you take it, I found some passages I thought were appropriate. If you like, I'll read them."

"Oh, Garth. Please do."

"Would you like a prayer first then the reading before we exchange our— our vows?"

'That would be lovely,'' Priscilla said, her heart suddenly warming. His boyish awkwardness astonished her as much as his unexpected thoughtfulness. Pleased, she smiled at him until his searching gaze brought a flush to her cheeks.

Silently Garth took the cup from her unsteady hand and laid it alongside his own. Then, facing her, he drew her to her knees while he, too, knelt. Their fingers intertwined, hers tingling, and when Garth bowed his head, Priscilla gladly followed suit.

"Father of heaven and earth," he prayed, "guide our words. Lead us in the true vows of wedlock in Christ's name." Her whispered 'amen' joined his.

"The verses I wanted to read are in Colossians," Garth said, "seventeen through nineteen."

" 'And whatever ye do in word or deed, do all in the name of the Lord Jesus, giving thanks to God and the Father by him. Wives, submit yourselves unto your own husbands, as it is fit in the Lord. Husbands, love your wives, and be not bitter against them.' "

Was Garth already bitter, Priscilla wondered, because she had refused to go with him as Laughing Owl had done? She had since regretted that hasty 'no,' but now there seemed no way of undoing it.

"Have you ever read the Song of Solomon?" Garth asked now, and Priscilla shook her head. But as Garth read from it, the words seemed prophetic.

" 'My beloved spoke, and said unto me, Rise up, my love, my fair one, and come away. For, lo, the winter is past, the rain is over and gone. The flowers appear on the earth; the time of singing of birds has come, and the voice of the turtledove is heard in our land.' "

"Garth, I—I . . . ." What could she tell him?

"It's all right, Priscilla," he said with surprising tenderness. "Maybe someday . . ." His voice drifted away, and his eyes returned to the pages still opened before him. "Ah, here's a verse for you in chapter four. " 'Behold, thou art fair, my love;' " he quoted, " 'behold, thou art fair. Thou hast doves' eyes.' " Suddenly he closed the leatherbound book, capturing her hands, her eyes, her breath as his intense gaze drew her to him.

"Do you, Priscilla, choose to be my wife, to have and to hold from this day forward until death do us part?"

"I do." Softly, she inhaled. "And do you, Garth, choose to be my husband—"

"—to have and to hold from this day forward until death do us part?" he said. "I do, Priscilla."

"Well?" she prodded.

"Patience, Little Dove. I presume you want me to say something like, 'By the power of God, I pronounce us husband and wife.' There! Will that do?"

It didn't sound exactly as she remembered, but Priscilla nodded. "That'll do." Then she insisted that they record their names and date of marriage in the Bible that Garth had provided.

That accomplished, he asked, "Now, do I get to kiss the bride?"

Timidly at first, she came into his arms, welcoming his brief kiss.

"Mrs. Daniels," he murmured against her cheek.

"Or Mr. Davis?" she teased.

"We'll compromise. The Wolf clan here, and the Daniels' name elsewhere."

"Agreed."

"Hmmm, I like it when you agree with me, Little Dove." His face nuzzled her cheek as he repeated, "Little Dove," softly. 'I hope the name suits without 'mourning.' "

Settled snugly against his chest, Priscilla suddenly stiffened. She could not, would not call Garth 'Bear Claw'. Did he expect that?

Apparently, he sensed her dilemma. "You'll need a new name for me, I suppose. Something like 'Sly Fox' or 'Mighty Oak,' " he said with a glimmer of amusement.

Priscilla laughed. "My! You certainly have an elevated opinion of yourself, sir," she said.

Leaning against him she twisted in his arms until she felt his warm breath on her forehead. "How about Running Deer?" she suggested "so you'll hurry home . . . to . . . me?" Her voice became a whisper as she realized what she had said.

His lips, brushing her forehead, halted. "A man would be a fool not to rush back to you," he said, but the words sounded grim.

Turning her round to him, his mouth bore down on hers urgently, as though he had not moments to spare. Priscilla responded, half in joy, half in sorrow. This was where she belonged, she thought; this was where she wanted to stay.

When Garth sat up and unfastened his shirt, the

loosened clothing exposed a dreadful scar, a welted cord that encircled his arm and brutally etched his side. Priscilla gasped.

Garth observed her coldly. "Repulsive, isn't it?"

Mute, her head shook with denial. It wasn't revulsion that she felt, but fear. That scar, that awful scar, had reminded her of Laughing Owl and Garth's deep love for her, a love that had given no thought even for his own life. He had told Priscilla about it, but seeing the scar now made that relationship dramatically clear. How could their own one-sided love begin to compare with what he had known before?

Closing her eyes, Priscilla attempted to remove the scar's intrusion from her thoughts. Garth was her husband now. She was his wife. Nothing else, no one else must matter.

When Garth turned to her, he had a cold look in his eye, as though he was hurt and would force her to think differently. But whatever thoughts she had had were driven from her instantly by panic as he reached for her. Words of protest chocked her, as she tried in vain to free herself from him. And when he finally released her, a terrifying eternity later, she found she was sobbing.

Garth sat up on the edge of the blankets, his back to her. When he spoke it was in dry tones. "Why didn't you tell me, Priscilla?"

"What difference would it make?" she countered through her sobs. She hadn't meant to snap at him, but she felt so humiliated.

He turned to look at her, his voice almost a hiss. "Did you and Charles ever—?"

"What do you think?" she interrupted, unable to bear hearing him speak so.

Garth gave a derisive laugh. "What do I think?" he mocked. "I think you either lied to me about the fact that you were married, or you're one of those prudish women who makes a man's life unbearable. Either way, it's contemptible."

"And, of course, you'd know. You're a judge, aren't you? Tell me, your honor, do you always convict the persons before you on such little evidence?"

"Well, what do you expect me to think?" Garth shot back.

"I don't know," she admitted wearily. "But don't punish me."

"Punish!" he exclaimed. "I assure you, madam, that no woman in my arms has wished to be elsewhere—until now."

Hurt and angry, she glared at him until he had the grace to look away. When he spoke again, she saw only his grim profile.

"I suppose it's your business, Priscilla, how you kept Charles away from you—or why. But don't expect the same consideration out of me," he warned. "You knew I wanted you before you consented to marry me."

"Oh, yes," she said. "You made it abundantly clear that that was the only reason you were marrying me."

Garth scowled. "Is that what you think?"

"What else is there?"

"Trust, caring, companionship," he bit off. "Why do you look so surprised? I'm human, Priscilla, regardless of what you think. Keep that in mind, will you, before *you* go convicting *me* on such little evidence."

For a moment, her crying subsided, thinking about what Garth had said. Perhaps they both had misjudged one another's motives and character, and, if so, their future held more promise than she would have dared believe. Hopeful, her eyes turned to him, flickering across his set jaw, his broad chest, his bare arm. There, her glance halted.

Garth followed it. "I'm sorry it bothers you," he said with disgust.

This time, however, Priscilla didn't look away. Instead she leaned closer, her hand reaching out to trace the reminder of his wounds, the reminder of Laughing Owl.

"You loved her very much," she said quietly. "I've never been loved like that."

"Good heavens! Is that what's troubling you?" Garth caught her hand. "Charles threw you that log, Priscilla. He cared."

"Charles never held me," she stated flatly, pulling back her hand.

Garth slid across the blanketed space between them and scooped her into his arms. "Forgive me, Little Dove," he whispered. "I thought my scars repulsed you. You're so exquisite, all that a man could hope for." His face nestled in her hair. "I didn't mean to hurt you." His low voice held unmistakable anguish. 'It never occurred to me that you . . . that this . . . It could be different," he finished awkwardly.

She believed him.

Toward dawn, she stirred, awakening to the charming lilt of a songbird. The fire had died to bright coals, and she wondered if she could give it a poke without disturbing Garth. He looked so peaceful. She decided not to chance it, but she snuggled deeper against him, seeking warmth.

Almost immediately, his arm coiled around her, drawing her closer. Priscilla laughed.

"I thought you were asleep."

"I was. You make it impossible to rest long."

Lazily, he lifted his thick lashes as he spoke, and now he stared at her with such longing, Priscilla gasped. Could that be love she saw? Last night, she had made no effort to hide her feelings for him, though she had not put them into words. She had even begun to believe that her love was not as one-sided as she had feared, and his present look confirmed the hope she had dared to cherish.

"Garth, let me go with you," she said recklessly.

"Where?" he teased.

She made a face. "Wherever it is you go."

Thoughtfully, he studied her. "You mean that, don't you?"

"I meant it the first time I said it," she declared. "And don't leap to conclusions. I *want* to go with you."

"I believe you do," he said astonished. But to her dismay, he shook his head. "I was only thinking of myself when I asked you, Little Dove. Believe me, it would never work."

"Why not?" she demanded peevishly. "I learn quickly. I could be a help to you."

He sighed.. "You're not used to this life and its hardships."

Impatiently she tossed her head. "Honestly, Garth, I'm not made of porcelain."

"Hmmmm." He seemed to give the matter some thought. "No, you're much too soft for porcelain."

His lips met hers, and he help her close until daylight had broken in upon them. Their heartbeats

106

seemed to keep pace with the rhythmic "kaboom" of the awakening village.

"You know, you're right," Garth said, as they rose to dress, "you do learn quickly."

"Oh? Then our lessons are complete," she teased.

"Never!" he exclaimed. Then, as though to show her, he leapt across the wavelet of blankets and swept her off her feet and into his arms.

## CHAPTER 8

THEY BREAKFASTED IN COMPATIBLE SILENCE. stealing
glances at one another, before they reluctantly parted
to do the day's chores. Priscilla hummed as she
pounded the corn and set soup to simmer by the fire.
Later, when she saw White Cloud and Straw Basket,
they responded to her glowing face with smiles.

Her bright mood stayed throughout the day, despite
Dancing Water's hostile glares. Priscilla spied the girl
by the stream as she dipped fresh water into her clay
pot. Understandably, the young woman seethed with
jealous anger, and while Priscilla felt a certain sympa-
thy, she determined not to let the girl's attitude affect
her.

She did, however, feel embarrassed by the giggles
and curious stares of the villagers who had witnessed
her collapse at the wedding ceremony. In time, she
hoped they would forget, for surely no typical bride of
the Aniyv-wiya would have behaved in such a fashion. The fainting spell had set her apart, which was

the direct opposite of what Priscilla had hoped to achieve by remaining in the village. Well, it couldn't be helped, she told herself, and eventually she would gain their trust and love. But, then and now, she was who she was, and the people would have to accept that or reject her altogether.

Which would Garth do, Priscilla wondered. At the present, he was obviously enamoured with her, yet he still had little confidence in her abilities. He had practically said as much when he had denied her the right to stay with him, going where he must go. Unless his opinion altered, he would soon grow weary of her inadequacies, seeing her as a liability, a burden, rather than the helpmeet God had intended a wife to be.

No, Priscilla vowed to herself, she would not let that happen. She wished she could easily and quickly prove herself, but she had learned from past experiences that forcing a matter, prematurely, generally produced disastrous results. She would have to bide her time, she knew, learning all that she could as well as she could, then leaving the rest to God. He was with her; He would guide.

Was He guiding her thoughts even now? As she sat fresh water on the fire to heat, Priscilla's thoughts kept returning to Nan-ye-hi, the Beloved Woman about whom she knew so little. Each time Garth had spoken her name, his voice, his tone, his expression conveyed the utmost respect for this daughter of the Wolf clan. Certainly, she was a woman to be admired, for had she not been elected to her sacred post by all the women of the nation?

Believing that Nan-ye-hi's life and character would hold a clue to the traits and manners most desired in a Cherokee woman, Priscilla determined to ask Garth about her. She sincerely prayed that she and the Beloved Woman of the nation would have something in common, something on which she could fasten her hopes of growing into the person, the wife Garth needed.

As soon as he entered their meager hut that evening, Priscilla demanded her husband to tell her all there was to know about Nan-ye-hi.

Immediately, Garth seemed amused. "Do I not first get a kiss?"

Priscilla blushed prettily and pecked her husband's cheek. "Now don't distract me, Garth," she scolded when he gathered her into his arms for a more thorough embrace. "I really want to know."

He laughed. "So I see." Yet he pulled her down with him on the blankets as he made himself comfortable.

Priscilla, however, was not to be deterred. "Didn't you tell me once that the Beloved Woman stayed by her husband's side, even in battle?" she asked with enthusiasm.

Nodding, Garth sighed. "But she isn't you, Priscilla."

"Of course not! But that doesn't mean we don't have some similarities. We're both of the Wolf clan," she insisted.

Garth snickered. "Yes, you are, Little Dove." Cradling her in his arms, he stroked her silken hair. "As a matter of fact, Nan-ye-hi was no older than you when she was elected to her position."

"Really?" Priscilla sat up, interested. "Tell me about it."

"It was about twenty years ago," Garth recollected, "sometime in the 1750's when she followed her husband, King Fisher, into one of the bloodiest battles ever seen in these parts."

"Who was fighting?" Priscilla interrupted.

"The Aniyv-wiya and Muskogeans as usual," Garth said grimly.

"Not whites?"

Garth shook his head. "We've had skirmishes, of course, and undoubtedly will again, but the true warring occurs between the various tribes. Eventually, I expect they will annihilate—or betray— one another."

"I hope not!" Priscilla exclaimed.

"Time will tell," Garth injected. "At any rate, the Taliwa battle was a particularly dreadful one. King Fisher had five-hundred men in his war party, but they were showing pretty poorly. Nan-ye-hi remained in the thick of it, crouched beside her husband. As he fired on the enemy, she hid behind a log, chewing his bullets."

"What?" Priscilla couldn't believe it.

"It's an old trick, actually," Garth confirmed. "Chewed bullets mangle the flesh with deadly results.

Priscilla shuddered. "Go on."

Garth smiled at her response before continuing. "Apparently, King Fisher's men were flagging badly, then he himself was wounded and killed. Nan-ye-hi didn't hesitate. She grabbed her husband's gun, reloaded, and joined the fight."

"If you believe the stories," Garth drawled on, "her actions that day rallied the men. The Aniyv-wiya won, and the Muskogeans moved out of the territory. Until then, they'd been quarreling over that spot for nigh onto forty years."

"Incredible!" Priscilla exclaimed. "All that because of one woman's bravery."

Garth chuckled. "I thought you would believe the stories. Now don't look at me with those dagger eyes. I agree. It's probably true. Nan-ye-hi is a remarkable woman."

"You've met her then?"

Garth nodded. "In Chota. I imagine you'll see her there when the village goes during the Green Corn Festival."

Priscilla gave a little clap. "I'd love that. Does she speak English?"

"I certainly hope so," Garth said dryly. "Her husband, Bryant Ward, is an Englishman."

"Really?" For some reason that surprised her.

"They have a daughter, Betsy, in addition to the two children Nancy and King Fisher bore."

"You called her Nancy," Priscilla noted.

"Nan-ye-hi, Nancy. The sound of her name was easily Anglicized, so you may hear her referred to as Nancy Ward."

"An ordinary name for such an extraordinary woman," Priscilla commented.

"Indeed. It's uncommon for one so young to be elected to the highest position of Beloved Woman," Garth said. "Regardless of who is presiding— Peace Chief or War Chief—Nancy sits with them near the ceremonial fire."

"Ah, but do they listen to her?" Priscilla had to ask.

Garth chuckled. "I assure you, if she speaks—and she often does, especially on matters of peace and social concerns—you can be certain that the good chiefs listen. It's thought, in fact, that the Great Spirit will use the Beloved Woman's voice to address the nation."

112

"The Great Spirit? You mean God?"

Garth nodded.

"Perhaps the people are right," Priscilla said almost to herself. "Perhaps God will use a woman's voice to address this nation."

She said nothing more on the subject, but it didn't leave her mind. Without his knowledge, Garth had confirmed the fact that she and the Beloved Woman had more in common than Priscilla had dared to hope—their willingness to remain at their husbands' side; their willingness to speak the words given them by God.

Priscilla doubted, however, that she would enjoy chewing Garth's bullets. She couldn't help but wonder though if Laughing Owl had ever done so, and asked her husband if he had yet found himself in need of chewed bullets. His response was a hearty laugh that relieved Priscilla's mind more than mere words.

"You might chew the leather for my feet," Garth suggested, playfully, "the next time I need moccasins."

Priscilla scalded him with her eyes as she ladled up their pottage.

They ate in silence—a smile playing all the while on Garth's lips. When they finished, he commented on the aptness of her cooking skills.

Priscilla hid her pride in the accomplishment behind a scolding. 'You needn't be so surprised," she admonished him. "Perhaps I'm more capable than you think, Garth Daniels!"

"I shan't argue that point," he chuckled as she started off with a toss of her head.

Without warning, he pulled her onto his lap.

"Garth!"

113

"Hush, Priscilla, and kiss me proper."

And she did.

Priscilla was steeped in the wonder of it all. Even her most cherished dreams had been bland compared to the reality of laying in Garth's arms. If only it could last; if only she could be with him always.

Too soon he left her, saying he would only be gone an hour or two. The town council met, regardless of one's preoccupation with love.

As soon as he left, Priscilla mused over her husband's comment that he was eager to return home to a passel of children. She hoped not to disappoint him, although she preferred a dark-haired, dark-eyed baby to the blonds he had set his heart on. How strange it would be to have a dove-eyed infant peering at her from his cradleboard. Would such a child be out of place? Charles had feared so. And he had feared, too, for Priscilla's own well-being.

Odd that two men could treat her so differently and have such differing concerns while both were men of God. Charles had believed her safe while traveling in his presence, and that had proved to be less than true. Garth, on the other hand, believed his wife's wellbeing rested in the protection of the village. Would that also be untrue? She had encountered no threats here, other than the ill will of Dancing Water, but separation from Garth was threat in itself.

Priscilla shuddered. She could not bear to think of days without her husband. Or nights. Yet she supposed she was safe enough—safer, at least than if she traveled among bears and warring tribes. Right now she would be of so little assistance to Garth, she couldn't blame him for refusing her accompaniment, but, Lord willing, that would change. She had learn to perform housewifely duties enough to gain his compliment, and her normal strength had returned now, increased. In time, she would be prepared, she hoped, to journey with him, alleviating his burdens rather than adding to them.

Meanwhile, she wondered how soon Garth would have to go? When she'd put the question to him, he had been vague in his reply, leading her to believe he felt no need for haste. Yet she knew he couldn't remain in a place too long. Thus far, he had been in the village longer than she. A day, a week, or two, and he would be compelled to leave, she supposed.

Garth had assured her, however, of his intermittent return. As he traveled back and forth to the white settlements and Indian towns scattered throughout the mountains, most trips would require no more than a fortnight. Such a schedule was tolerable—and possible because her husband had had the foresight to build his stock adequately before their marriage. Priscilla appreciated that, but within the year, he would have to augment those supplies, taking a trip back East to do so. Then he would be away for months, instead of days, and even three months sounded a lifetime.

She wondered what Garth would say about her accompanying him on that long trip. She could see her family again. And meet his. The idea elated her the more she thought about it, and by the time Garth had returned from the council meeting, Priscilla was convinced her plan would suit him fine.

She presented it cheerfully, but his reaction failed to equal her optimism.

"We'll see," he said, noncommitally.

'But, Garth!" she pressed him. "You must consider the matter."

He raised a wary eyebrow. "Must I?"

She took no heed of his cautioning glance. "I want to meet your family." She stamped her foot. "And I want you to meet mine."

"Why, Prissy? To gain the favor of parental consent?" he asked, scornfully. "It's a bit late for that, don't you think?"

"Must you always twist my meaning?" she shot back. "I'm curious, that's all, and I thought perhaps that you'd be too."

When he said nothing, Priscilla's temper rose. "Pardon me, sir. I see I'm mistaken about your interest in me. Apparently, it's as I first supposed."

"What are you saying?" Garth asked darkly.

"I should think that would be obvious," she said haughtily. "You fancy me, and nothing more."

Garth sighed heavily. "You'll think what you wish regardless of what I say, Priscilla. I'm tired, and I'm going to bed. Are you coming or not?"

"Not."

"Suit yourself," he said, undressing.

"I'm too agitated to sleep."

"Well, you needn't be." Garth poked the fire before lying down. Immediately, he closed his eyes. "There's unrest among some of the white settlers, Priscilla. As long as you don't venture from the people of this village, you've no cause to worry." He spoke in a monotone. "I'll assess the situation again before I travel East. That's all I can promise you."

It took a moment for Priscilla to realize that was all she had asked— for Garth to consider the matter. She realized too that she had done the very thing she had intended *not* to do—force the issue prematurely— and by doing so, she had been rewarded with the disastrous results she wanted to avoid. If only she had kept her lips sealed, she chided herself. By pressing the issue beyond a mere inquiry, she had goaded him and he her.

Silently, she watched his thick lashes fluttering against his cheeks before settling down to sleep. How handsome, how innocent her husband looked in his repose. He had seen no need to address himself to her accusation, and now Priscilla regretted making it. Garth did care; he did show concern for her far beyond fancy.

She supposed she owed him an apology. Or a word of gratitude for his promise to consider taking her back East. But he looked so peaceful, she didn't wish to disturb him.

Quietly, she prepared herself for bed, and she slipped beneath the blanket, snuggling close to him. Lightly, she kissed his cheek, a peace offering. Immediately, his eyes flew open.

"I thought you were sleeping."

"I thought you weren't."

Her apology slipped away, replaced with kisses.

Suddenly, Garth chuckled. "Careful, Mrs. Daniels," he said, "or I'm apt to think you fancy me and nothing more."

Priscilla made a face. "Do be quiet, Garth, and kiss me," she said. And he did, long into the starlit night.

## CHAPTER 9

GARTH STAYED A MONTH LONGER. By then, the village fields had been planted, a task that taxed Priscilla's strength to the limit. Each night, she sank wearily into bed, and each morning, she awakened groggily.

"I think you'll be glad to have me gone a fortnight," Garth commented when she nearly fell asleep in his arms.

But she wasn't glad. She was miserable, and the sun rose with such burdens, she began to wonder if she were ill again. Her shoulders drooped, her steps lagged until even Dancing Water noticed.

"I see Bear Claw has taken away your heart," the girl sneered. "Do not say I did not warn you."

As she bent over her day's wash, Priscilla felt too tired to argue with the girl. Ignoring her, she scrubbed a spot on a garment against the flat-topped rock she had chosen by the edge of the stream. Her arms ached as she rubbed, and her head felt light.

Dancing Water drew closer, watching her until

Priscilla could feel the girl's dark eyes boring. Around them, the chatter of the other women quieted as though they were waiting for something to happen. Heedless, Priscilla scrubbed on.

"Have you nothing to say?" Dancing Water demanded. When Priscilla didn't answer, the girl went on. "I have words! We do not want you here. Bear Claw was mine, and you have driven him away."

Reluctantly, Priscilla glanced up at the malevolent face above her.

"Perhaps your spiteful tongue drove him away from you," she couldn't help but say.

Although true, the statement incensed Dancing Water. With a shriek, the girl lunged forward, knocking Priscilla into the stream. Panic assailed her temporarily, for she knew she was no match for the younger woman. Even if she were, she certainly did not wish to come to blows amidst the rocks.

Backing away, Priscilla threw out her arm, gesturing, "Halt!" before the girl could leap on her again. Dancing Water, however, paid her no mind. She charged ahead, pushing Priscilla to the bottom of the stream and holding her there until the other women yanked the girl away, scolding her.

Choking and gasping for breath, Priscilla sat upright, glad for the work-roughened hands that held her in place. Two other women held back Dancing Water, who strained and jerked within their grasp.

"Your friends will not stop me again," Dancing Water warned.

Priscilla flung her wet hair from her face and met the girl's icy stare that chilled her far more than the mountain stream.

"Harm me if you wish, Dancing Water, but you'll

only make Bear Claw dislike you more. And, if my blood stains your hand, you'll force him to bring you harm."

Angrily, Dancing Water glared at her. "He was mine until you came."

"Was he? Do not be so certain of that," Priscilla said with more calmness than she felt. "Regardless, he is not yours now. He is my husband, and you must accept that."

To her astonishment, the girl laughed. "Husband! In our village, Bear Claw has but to take his possessions and go to be done with you. Has he not already?"

"You know he hasn't," Priscilla retorted. "You know his work takes him away, just as your men must go during the long hunt. Besides," she added, "we are married not only according to your customs. We are married according to the laws that we uphold—laws that are not so easily broken."

The dark eyes narrowed as Dancing Water refused to give in. "I know something of your law," she smugly maintained. "I know of the civil ceremony that occurred when Nan-ye-hi married her man, Ward. She herself has told me. Did you have such a ceremony? Tell me. Did you?"

Shivering from something other than the cold water, Priscilla rose, unsteadily, from the stream.

"My husband is a judge, a man of the law," she said with dignity. "He performed our civil ceremony in the privacy of our home."

"Did he?" Dancing Water scoffed. "Then show me."

"Show you?" Priscilla repeated quizzically. "Oh, I see. You want proof."

It was a simple enough request, Priscilla supposed, especially if it would lay the girl's mind to rest. She would not, however, allow Dancing Water to bully her. "Very well. As soon as I have finished my wash, I will show you."

Without waiting for the girl's response, Priscilla splashed about in the water, until she retrieved the garment she had been washing. When she found it, she examined the cloth for damage with slow deliberation. Then she wrung out the dress and scrubbed it again until she was satisfied.

Dancing Water waited impatiently, but Priscilla did not give her a glance. Chin jutted forward, she scrambled up the bank, taking time to squeeze the water out of the dress she wore. Each twist and turn of the fabric calmed her further, and at last she headed toward her hut, not bothering to see if the girl had followed.

A series of splashes and chattering from behind told Priscilla that more than one woman had tagged along. Apparently those sympathetic toward her sensed the tensions that still existed and had come to lend their support— or enjoy a good fight. Regardless, she strode purposefully ahead until she had reached the entrance of her hut. There she stopped, turning to face Dancing Water and the other women.

"Wait here," she said, holding up an arm bent to stop their entry. This was her home, and she wanted no malice within its walls.

The faces peering in, however, did not bother her. Naturally, the women were curious about her, and it pleased Priscilla that they should find a well-kept hut, much like their own. The clay pots were scrubbed, the dirt floor swept clean, and the fire well-laid. The smell

121

of bubbling soup filled the room as Priscilla crossed it, going to a corner shelf that Garth had constructed.

Atop the rough oak plank lay the Bible her husband had given to her on their wedding night. Carefully, Priscilla took down the leather-bound volume, pressing it tightly against her bosom. She had been so glad when Garth gave her the cherished book, but she had never expected such an unusual opportunity for showing it to some of the village women, especially not with Dancing Water, the instigator, among them. God certainly knew how to turn ill to good, she thought.

Smiling at the humor of the situation, she crossed back to the entrance of the hut.

"This is the Bible, our holy book." Priscilla held up the volume so that all of the women could see. "These pages are sacred to my people because they tell of the living God and His Son, Jesus. The book contains the laws of God and His promises, and it also has the stories, poems, and wise sayings of His people."

As she spoke, Priscilla directed her words to Dancing Water, who now interrupted. "Do not tell me that this book speaks of you and Bear Claw," the girl scoffed.

Priscilla smiled. "I was not going to say that, although the Bible does speak with such complete truth that every person on earth can recognize himself or herself in the stories. Even you, Dancing Water."

Seeing the girl's disbelief, Priscilla hastened on. "When a man and woman marry, it is our custom to write down the names and date in this holy book."

"Show me," Dancing Water commanded.

"As you wish," Priscilla said, opening the leather cover. How glad she was that she had insisted on recording their marriage immediately.

Leafing through, she quickly found the page, her fingers lingering over their inscribed names. Above them, someone had written the names of Garth's parents and their wedding date, and in between, his birth was recorded. The lower half of the page stood empty, awaiting future births and marriages to be penned in along the provided lines.

Priscilla held up the record for all curious eyes to see.

"You know, of course," she said to Dancing Water, "that Bear Claw has an English name, Garth Daniels, and mine is Priscilla."

The girl nodded slightly.

"Here. On this line, it says 'Garth Edlin Daniels married Priscilla Davis Prescott', and then it gives the date, in the year of our Lord," Priscilla explained, pointing.

"What is written there?" Dancing Water asked as she indicated a line above.

It says that Richard Garth Daniels married Elizabeth Margaret Edlin in 1733." Priscilla answered. "They are Garth's—Bear Claw's—parents," she went on to explain.

Suddenly, Dancing Water grabbed the leather Bible from Priscilla's unsuspecting hands, carelessly flipping the pages, almost to the end of the book. Then, she thrust the open volume back to its owner.

"Tell me these words," the girl demanded, stoutly tapping the thin paper with her forefinger.

"Very well," Priscilla agreed. She laid her finger on the exact location of Dancing Water's sound tap, following each word with the movement of her hand as she read.

" 'Every good gift and every perfect gift is from

above, and cometh down from the Father of Lights, with whom is no variation, either shadow of turning.'" Priscilla read. "That's from the first chapter of James, and . . ."

Again Dancing Water yanked the book away. This time, she flipped the pages back where they settled on Romans, chapter thirteen.

"Say these words," she insisted, giving the eighth verse a solid thump.

Calmly, Priscilla retrieved her Bible, reading once again with her finger underlining each word.

"'Owe no man any thing, but to love one another; for he that loveth another hath fulfilled the law.'"

Dancing Water turned away.

'Wait!" Priscilla called. "Don't you want me to read more?"

"I have heard enough," the girl said, her proud face gleaming. "Your book speaks of love as law. That too is the way of my people. I love Bear Claw. He is mine!"

Triumphantly, Dancing Water marched off with the other women trailing behind. Stunned at this turn of events, Priscilla stood in the doorway, gaping after them. Whatever she had thought to accomplish with the girl had been defeated. And, worse, Dancing Water could interpret the scriptures any way she wanted to the others since she was the only one who had understood the language.

But she didn't understand! The girl had merely twisted the words of the Bible to suit her own purpose, and Priscilla felt dismayed—shocked—that she had been the instrument of such deception.

Feeling shaken, she retreated to the dark interior of the hut where she settled herself by the low-burning fire. With her Bible on her lap, she opened the book, leafing through until she located the seventeenth verse she had read aloud from the first chapter of James. That phrase "shadow of turning" had stayed in her mind, and she sensed now that the words had some message of comfort.

She read it again to herself and then again. And then she read the entire chapter to be sure she had understood the full context and meaning. The Father of Light does not vary from light to dark. The Father of Light is not overshadowed. The Father of Light sends only good.

Satisfied, Priscilla closed the Bible and cradled it against her. She had no idea what good gift could come from this day, but she knew now that it would. God was in charge, and He brought no darkness. Anything shadowed that would happen could be looked on as a temporary inconvenience, she told herself.

Trials, ill circumstance, misunderstandings, even death—they were all like a misty shroud that separated the known from the unknown, Priscilla thought. Until recently, she had perceived whatever situation she found herself in as being what was real, what was known. But as her faith in God had grown, her thinking had reversed. God was real; His love and power were knowable. And all that could be felt, seen, heard, touched, or tasted, was either a convenience or an inconvenience, great or small.

How simple it was during those times when veiled thoughts parted, giving her a glimpse of God's reality—His purpose—overtaking what *seemed* to be happening. Then, everything made perfect sense. At the moment, however, little did. And Priscilla could only trust that God knew what He was doing. She certainly didn't know! And Dancing Water *seemed* to be more of a problem than ever.

Over the next few days though, the girl attended to her own business, aloof but somewhat less hostile than usual. Priscilla felt relieved, deciding not to question the matter further.

During the daylight hours, she planned her work to coincide as often as possible with the routines of Straw Basket or White Cloud. Their companionship offered a kind of strength that helped Priscilla through the lonely time while Garth was away. From them, she also learned new skills that she hoped would please him—weaving, herbal cooking, gardening— the latter of which including flapping one's arms in the fields to scare away the *go-gv*, crow.

And so the days passed in waiting. Waiting for the Three Sisters to grow. Waiting for Dancing Water to make another move. Waiting for Garth to come home. Waiting for God's purpose to be made known.

Keeping busy helped Priscilla to fill the hours while keeping thoughts at bay. But, thanks to Dancing Water, one niggling worry took root, then grew: Were she and Garth really married? She honestly didn't know.

At the time, she had been so caught up in the drama of the day that any vows exchanged and scriptures read seemed more binding than merely trading ears of corn for the leg of a deer. Surely the promises they had made meant more than the tying of two blankets. But was that true? Did familiar customs make their marriage legal while unfamiliar customs did not? Somehow she didn't think so.

Unfortunately, Priscilla had never witnessed a civil

126

ceremony of marriage, so she had nothing with which to compare. Her own marriage to Charles had been under the auspices of the church with nothing unusual about the service except their haste in seeing it performed. Of course, her family members had been absent from that occasion, but Charles' uncles had deigned to give her away—his reluctance due to the inevitable wrath he'd have to meet when Priscilla's father returned from England. Understandable. But even so, the extraordinary circumstances of that day made it no less legal. She and Charles were securely married, according to the laws of God and of the crown.

Was that true now? Had she and Garth satisfied the laws which they esteemed? He had said he was a judge, but was he? This was a wilderness territory as far as their people were concerned, not a 'civilized' colony. Perhaps Garth had no jurisdiction here. If not, she had been living with a man outside of wedlock! Oh, what would Lettie say to that?

What would God say? Oddly enough, Priscilla didn't think He would mind. There had been no pastors or priests in the days of Abraham, yet he and other patriarchs of old simply took a woman for a wife. Jurisdiction belonged to God, if not to Garth, and surely He knew their vows had been sincere.

". . . for he that loveth another hath fulfilled the law."

Priscilla laughed, remembering the verse from Romans that had convinced Dancing Water that Bear Claw was hers. That same verse offered a measure of hope now. Even if she and Garth were not married according to the laws of the crown, their marriage could be binding in God's eyes, couldn't it? She loved her husband and had reason to believe he loved her. Under normal circumstances, that, of course, would not suffice, but these were not normal circumstances. The nearest preacher was in the Watauga settlement, if that good reverend had yet returned.

Priscilla wondered if one might find a justice of the peace there? Oh, why hadn't she thought of that sooner? She scolded herself severely, but that did nothing to alter the situation that, each day, seemed to grow worse. Garth had not returned to alleviate her fears, and she began to suspect that she had been deceiving herself as Dancing Water had done.

Her husband had said he would be back in a fortnight, and already it was beyond that. The corn had begun to grow, blades bursting through the well-tended soil, green leaves stalking daily towards the sky. Warming, the days had lengthened along with the corn until the spare hours of sunlight invited the villagers to play. Often, Priscilla collapsed onto her corn-husk mattress at dusk, falling into a restless sleep while the ground beneath her quaked with stomping feet, dancing as accompanying chants beat the air.

Usually, however, she fell asleep reading the Bible that Garth had given her. Over and over again she read the thirteenth chapter of Romans, then devoured the whole book before returning to dissect, word by word, the eighth verse. That then necessitated putting each piece back into context until she arrived at some conclusion, which, unfortunately, the next day, she would question. Exhausted by the effort, Priscilla finally turned the matter over to God, asking Him to instruct her and guide her, even as she slept.

The following morning, she awoke feeling more

refreshed than she had in some time, and three things had become immediately clear. The first thing was that God had created the law through Moses, and therefore He condoned it. The second was that God had created His Son to bring forth love into the world —forgiving, accepting, caring love that wished no harm on other people and therefore kept the law by its very nature.

Priscilla had no difficulty with either of those clear thoughts, but the third proved more weighty. Although she was convinced now that she and Garth were married according to God's laws and their own binding promises, that did not make them married in the eyes of others. As long as another person—be it Dancing Water or Lettie or a future offspring—had cause to doubt the validity of that ceremony, she and Garth were acting as a stumbling block. Love would not behave in such a fashion. Love would not cause Dancing Water to covet or Lettie to curse or a child to remain forever nameless!

She and Garth would have to repeat their vows, properly this time, with witnesses and a pastor or justice of the peace. She hoped he would understand that, and more importantly, she hoped he truly wanted her—Priscilla Davis Prescott Daniels—for his wife.

Priscilla wanted that for herself, of course, but she especially wanted that for her children, her child. It was much too soon to be certain, but she felt confident that Garth's wish would be forthcoming in the not too distant future. Blond and gray-eyed or brunette, a baby, Priscilla thought, was on the way.

## CHAPTER 10

PRISCILLA PLUCKED A WEED from the garden and twirled it in her fingers. The color and shape of the leaves was so similar to the actual shoots of corn that a careless eye would be unable to discern the difference. Practice had taught her to recognize the quality, the texture of the genuine plant that would someday bear fruit and living seed. The weed, however, would propogate its own kind and nothing more, but left untended, it had the power to drain the needed nutrients from that which gave food and life to the village.

As she tossed away the deceiving plant, a movement on the far edge of the garden caught her eye.

"Garth!"

Immediately Priscilla straightened from the patch she had set out to hoe. Then, dropping her rough utensil of wood and stone, she sped across the garden and flung herself into Garth's outstretched arms.

"Miss me?" he asked, whirling her around until she was dizzy.

Her answer was a kiss that left her gasping for breath.

"Put me down, Garth," she pleaded when a little girl's giggles reached her ears. "No Cherokee wife would greet her husband so publicly."

Garth laughed. "I expect you're right, my love," he said, putting her onto unsteady feet, "but it's been too long since I've held you to exercise restraint."

"Where have you been?"

"Obviously detained," Garth said, dropping a light kiss onto the tip of her dirt-smudged nose. "Come on. Let's talk in our hut."

"But—but I have work to do," she hesitated.

"It's nothing that can't wait, dear wife. The garden will be here later, and so, no doubt, will the weeds."

"Go ahead, then. I'll just be a moment. I must fetch my hoe."

Her husband strode away as Priscilla hurried back to get the hoe. How lighthearted she felt, and so much the bride, now that Garth was home. Still, uneasiness tugged as she retraced her steps, for in the distance Garth stood talking to Dancing Water.

The discussion appeared animated. Not wishing to disturb it, Priscilla slipped around the edge of the village, swiftly reaching the sanctity of her home. Home! Barren, mud-plastered walls and a roof with a hole in it. But as long as she and Garth shared the dwelling, their life and their memories made the meager place special.

She wished he would hurry to her as she had to him. But now she paced the room, clasping and unclasping her hands as she waited for her husband to appear. When he did come in, he was scowling.

"Prissy, did you tell Dancing Water that we're not married?"

"What?" It seemed impossible to think with him frowning at her so!

"Did you?" he repeated.

"Of course not!"

"Well, for some reason," Garth said, "she has it in her head that I'm free to commit myself to her."

"That's ridiculous, and she knows it," Priscilla said, frowning. "What did you say?"

"I told her I had a wife and that was that, but she didn't seem to take me too seriously," Garth admitted. "I don't understand what brought on her bold display of affection, Priscilla, but I assure you, I did nothing to encourage her."

Priscilla smiled in spite of herself. Dancing Water's behavior was no laughing matter, but her husband's bewilderment was charming—almost the air of an innocent child falsely accused.

"I believe you, Garth," Priscilla said. "If there are confessions to make, I fear it is I who must make them."

As lightly as she could, she skimmed over the incident at the stream that precipitated the need to provide Dancing Water with proof of their marriage.

"I felt the Lord had arranged that very moment as an opportunity for me to share His name," Priscilla went on, "for the other women followed us here out of curiosity. I explained briefly what the Bible is and how it was our custom to record marriages within its cover. I showed Dancing Water our names, and then, before I knew what was happening, she had jerked the book away and was demanding that I read to her the verses to which she pointed."

Even before Garth asked, Priscilla headed toward the oak shelf. Then, getting down the Bible, she read the verses to him. When she finished, she looked up and found her husband staring thoughtfully into the fire.

"Hmmmm. I believe I understand," he said at last. "Dancing Water is also one to take full advantage of an opportunity."

"If that's meant to set me in my place," Priscilla said, feeling admonished, "I assure you it's not necessary. I've rued the moment more than you'll ever know. In fact, it's caused me no little distress."

To her surprise, Garth took her into his arms. "I've no wish to accuse you, Priscilla," he said, his lips brushing her forehead. "I'm sorry you've suffered over this matter, but I believe it will work out for the best, as you first intended."

"I hope so," she said glumly.

"Trust me. I'll take care of Dancing Water," Garth promised.

Tilting up her chin, he kissed the dimple he found there. "You're trembling," he said. "Is something else troubling you?"

Priscilla chewed her lower lip. She had waited for endless days for her husband's return, and now his very presence set her aquiver. But the concerns that Dancing Water had stirred up needed to be laid to rest.

Reluctantly, she freed herself from Garth's embrace.

"There *is* something disturbing you," he said.

Priscilla nodded. "It's about the legality of our marriage," she said, haltingly. "Dancing Water's questions made me wonder, well . . ."

Her explanations stopped as she saw the tightening of Garth's jaw.

"I thought you were satisfied," he said almost coldly.

"I was! I mean, I am. But there are other people to consider."

A dark eyebrow rose in disdain. "Prissy, did it ever occur to you that you concern yourself entirely too much with what other people will think?"

"Perhaps one of us should," she returned hotly. "I suppose it makes little difference to you, Garth, but I prefer that our marriage be a witness, an example rather than a stumblingblock."

Garth seemed somewhat amused. "And who, pray tell, is stumbling on our account?"

"Dancing Water, for one."

The amusement vanished. "I told you I'd take care of her."

"What about our families, then?"

"Ah! I thought as much." Garth gave an ironic laugh. "Are they your conscience, Prissy? Are they looking over your shoulder these many miles away?"

"Don't be ridiculous. I'm quite capable of making up my own mind."

"Really?" His dark eyes swept over her. "Shall we put a wager on that?"

She frowned, not knowing what he meant.

"Before the year is out, I shall seek your father's permission for your hand. I'll ask his blessing on our marriage. But," Garth went on, "if such is not forthcoming, Priscilla, I wager that you'll be gone before I can say farewell."

Priscilla stared at him, incredulous. "Is that what you think? Seek what you will, but Charles and I had no such permission or blessing."

"What?" Garth did not believe her.

134

"It wasn't as I wished, of course," Priscilla explained patiently. "Papa was away, Mama was abed, and Lettie refused to come to the wedding."

"But why? I thought you and Charles had known one another all your lives."

"We had. We were the best of friends."

"But nothing more?" Garth finished for her.

"That depends on how you view it," Priscilla said. "We felt the Lord was calling us here, and little else mattered."

"And so you submitted yourself to a marriage of convenience," Garth said wryly. "How very noble of you, Prissy."

"Oh, be quiet," she said. "You don't know what you're talking about."

"I know that it's perfectly natural for a man and woman who are married to desire one another, my dear. God Himself ordained it. Perhaps you and Charles should have considered that aspect of marriage before you leapt into wedlock."

"You make our vows sounds paltry. It wasn't like that at all, Garth Daniels. For your information, Charles was quite interested in me, but being a man of scruples, he had no wish to burden me with a—a child in the middle of a wilderness."

To her astonishment, Garth gave a slight bow. "If Charles were here, I'd beg his pardon for questioning his mettle."

"And well you should," Priscilla exclaimed. "Charles at least gave a care to the welfare of his family."

"What's that supposed to mean?" Garth asked darkly.

"That you should do the same, perhaps." Priscilla

135

flung her hands about as though to whisk away Garth's anger. She had not intended to ignite his temper, but even now she couldn't let the subject drop—not when the consequences held such significance.

"What if we have children, Garth?" she asked at last. "Is it enough for us to tell them that we're married? Or do we owe them that assurance legally? It's not for myself, you understand," she hastened to add, "for I believed then and now that our vows were acceptable. But I question the legalities of our ceremony. Surely even a judge has limited jurisdiction."

"I never said I was a judge, Priscilla."

"You—you what?"

Garth sighed deeply. Then he sat down, his elbows on his knees, his hands wearily clasping his forehead.

"The appointment came, but I didn't accept it," he said. "If you'll recall, I never said that I did."

"You knew very well that I would assume so!" Priscilla exclaimed. "Oh, Garth, how could you?"

"How could I what?" he responded with feeling. "You would never have married me otherwise, and I couldn't leave you alone here unless you did."

"Have I no say in the matter? How dare you make such a momentous decision for me without consulting me, without supplying me with the facts!" Priscilla wrung her hands. To think she had trusted him. For what?

Saying nothing, she paced the room. With each step, the agony and frustration mounted until she thought she would scream. She wanted to hit him, to throw something, to tear this hut apart.

"Calm down, Priscilla," Garth said at last.

She stopped her pacing and looked at him. "Calm

down? Oh, really, Garth, you're the most obtuse man I've ever met. Have you no heart? You've just informed me that our marriage is a fraud, and then you expect me to react calmly?"

"Of course not, but you needn't be so shocked. You yourself questioned the legality of our ceremony."

"Only from the standpoint of others," she returned. "As for myself, I thought, I thought . . . ." To her dismay, she sank on the corn-husk mattress and burst into tears.

Garth neared and slipped an arm around her, but Priscilla wrenched away from his touch. She found no comfort now in his embrace.

Slamming a fist into the mattress, Garth backed away. "Tell me what you thought," he demanded.

Without looking at him, she asked, "What difference does it make?"

"I don't know," he answered truthfully. "But tell me anyhow."

She sniffed, still refusing to meet his gaze. "I thought our vows were genuine and well-intentioned. It never occurred to me that yours were spoken with full knowledge of deceit."

It was like the weeds growing beside the Three Sisters, Priscilla thought —so similar to what was real, so convincing, and yet nothing good could ever come of the deception. Was their marriage also to be recognized as mimicry with no hopes of becoming a genuine union, fruitful in love?

She held her breath, waiting for Garth's reply, for it seemed that he had the power to pluck and twirl and toss away their marriage far more than she. She had committed herself to him in thought and vow and deed, and now there was no turning back, especially if a child were on the way. Regardless, she had loved him—still loved him—and would love his child fiercely, proudly. But if unwed in his eyes she would not allow this man to touch her again.

Garth's voice cut into her thoughts. "I meant our vows, Priscilla. I doubt that you'll believe me, but I had only your best interests at heart." He stopped himself. "No, that's not precisely true. I had my interests in mind, too, but I never wanted to deceive you. Oddly enough, though you may not believe me, I merely wanted to relieve you of worry, to assure you that you had a home, a husband, a place here in this village where you seemed so determined to be.

"I confess, however," he continued, "that I lack Charles' foresight. I want a family. I've told you that. But I gave no thought to a reversal of our situation should we ever return to society. Our children would be the object of ridicule and confusion if we were not properly wed. I should not want them or you to be subjected to such ill treatment, Priscilla, any more than I wanted you to be subjected to it here."

Priscilla supposed she should be grateful for her husband's willingness to protect her, but her eyes misted as she sought his face. He had spoken sincerely; of that she was sure. But he had failed to mention the one quality she had most desired—love.

"Will you forgive me?" he asked.

Unable to trust her voice, she merely nodded.

"What would you have me do now, Priscilla? You need only to toss my possessions outside of this hut, and the villagers will no longer consider us wed. You would be free then to do as you like."

"And what would you do?" she asked as soon as she had found her voice. "Marry someone else?"

"No." He sounded annoyed. "There's no one else. I thought I had made that clear, Priscilla. I want you."

"Then I'll not turn you out," she stated firmly. "Let the Aniyv-wiya think we're married. The arrangement suits me—as you knew it would."

Garth moved toward her, but Priscilla put out a staying hand. "Please don't touch me," she begged.

"Why not? I thought you had forgiven my poor judgment."

"So I have. But we must think ahead."

"Priscilla, I only wanted to hold you."

"I—I'm sorry, Garth. I thought—"

"I know what you thought. But let me tell you something, Prissy. As long as we're in this camp, we are indeed legally married. The laws here are the ones we must submit to, not those someplace else. So unless you're willing to throw me out of this hut I have every right to expect you to act as my wife. Do I make myself clear?"

"Perfectly."

"Good. Then I'm going for a walk." He went out without another word.

Priscilla sat staring at his retreating back. He was right, she knew, though she didn't care to admit it. She wanted it both ways, which was not exactly fair to Garth. He had said, of course, that he had no intention of marrying anyone else, and Priscilla had no doubts that he did want her in the strictest physical sense. But was that enough for either of them? In time, she expected, emotions would ebb. And then what? Bitterness? Resentment? The frustration of feeling trapped in a loveless marriage?

Shamefully, Priscilla knew now she had had no business marrying Charles without loving him as a person, a lover, a friend. Anything less would sour eventually. Theirs had been a marriage of convenience, regardless of their purposes, and she could not—would not—repeat such a mistake with Garth.

When he came home that evening, silent and withdrawn, she quietly prepared his meal of ga-du, soup, and fresh-picked berries. Then she moved slowly to his side, wrapping her arms around him.

"Priscilla, what are you doing?"

"Acting as your wife!"

"Well, stop it."

"Stop? But you said—"

"I know what I said," he cut in, "but forget it. Get some rest, Priscilla. I'll be gone in the morning."

"Gone? For how long?"

"I don't know."

"But why?"

"It's best this way, don't you see? Being near you is torment."

"But I've been thinking about what you said, Garth, and you're right. The law of the Aniyv-wiya is the only law we have at present."

"At present, yes, but there's the future to consider, as you so aptly pointed out."

"So where does that leave us?" she asked bitterly. "With a marriage of convenience—for my sake? Well, I won't have it—for you or me, Garth! God forgive me for ever thinking otherwise."

It was hard to see with tears salting down her eyes, but heedless, Priscilla stumbled about the room, snatching up one of Garth's garments, then another.

"What are you doing?" Garth demanded.

"What does it look like?" she snapped as she began to throw his possessions out the door.

"You can't do this!"

"Can't I? Watch me," she said, grabbing up his pouch and hurling it, too, outside.

"Stop this, Priscilla!" he commanded. "You don't know what you're doing."

"I know exactly what I'm doing," she raged as she tossed out the last of his belongings. "I'm freeing us, Garth—both of us—to have a *true* marriage based on commitment and love. That's the way it has to be. Anything else is a fraud."

"Listen, Priscilla," he said in a voice that seemed, to her, patronizing. "It's not too late to restore appearances here."

"Appearances! How dare you talk to me about appearances, Garth Daniels. You've done nothing but ridicule mine ever since I've been here. Calling me Prissy, mocking me, questioning my motives, criticizing my background. Well, I'll not have it, do you hear? Whether I'm at home or in this village, I do the best I can to accept my surroundings, regardless of personal feelings or discomfort, and you might give some credit instead of—of *sniggering* at me."

"I've never sniggered," Garth said, while a smile played havoc with one corner of his mouth.

"Then stop accusing me of caring too much what other people think, on the one hand, and cautioning me about appearances on the other."

"That's not what I meant," he said, exasperated. "When I leave here, I want to know that you have the protection of our marriage. Can't you at least give me that peace of mind?"

"Why should I?"

"Because," he answered carefully, 'I think you love me. Tell me, Priscilla. Am I wrong?"

Garth stood in the doorway, complying with her need for distance. He had spoken softly to the back that Priscilla had turned to him, but when she did not respond, he repeated sharply, "Tell me if I'm wrong."

Priscilla wheeled around. "No, you're not wrong, and you know it! There. I hope you're satisfied, Garth Daniels, because I'm not. Yes, I love you. I've said it, and I want nothing less from you. So just go away— please —and leave me alone before I scream and bring down the whole village."

"That would be most unwise," he cautioned, "because then we would have to go through the entire ceremony again before I would leave. Close your mouth, Priscilla. I mean what I say! That's better. I'll gather my belongings now and be off before anyone is the wiser, and you'll give me the peace of mind I so desire while I'm away. Understood?" He waited for her answer.

"All right! Now go."

"I'm going, though I detest leaving you when you're quite beyond reason. Perhaps when you've soothed yourself, you'll realize that—"

"Garth! Would you just leave?"

"I'm leaving," he assured her calmly. "But believe me, Mrs. Daniels, I will be back."

## CHAPTER 11

PRISCILLA STOOD IN THE DOORWAY of her hut, looking in the direction of the mountains. Today their gentle peaks hid behind layers of smoky clouds that obscured the view she knew was there. How often she had gazed upon the summits and watched their subtle change from the new yellow-green of spring to the deeper, richer colors of summer. Yet despite the changing shades and hues, the majestic peaks remained the same, regardless of the seasons or the clouds or the fickle weather, and from them Priscilla had drawn strength.

God, too, remained the same. His strength, above all, could be trusted. The peaks of His power, the summits of His love would not be long obscured.

At the moment, however, they were. At the moment, that dreary veil had draped itself once again between the knowing and the not knowing, the believing and the not believing that all would be well. All *was* well, she reminded herself, whether it seemed to be so or not.

Even that reassurance, however, failed to banish the clouds. They still hovered, and she still hurt. Although she had no doubt that God was there working good in her life, she could not help the bleak feelings and the heaviness of her heart. Garth was gone, she wasn't married, and she would be a mother before the next breath of spring.

A fine kettle of fish, Lettie would say. Priscilla supposed it was that and more. Admittedly she had gotten herself into these circumstances, yet she couldn't believe she acted totally on impulse or totally alone. She had sought God's direction for her life in openness and good conscience, and even though she felt miserable and alone, she couldn't regret her choices. She loved Garth; she was glad she married him; and she was glad she carried his child.

In the weeks since he left, she was especially glad that he had protected her from her own rash behavior in tossing him out—although, at the time, she felt that, too, was right. She had wanted him to understand clearly, once and for all, that she never had intentions of using him. She supposed she had made her point, for Garth at least accepted the fact of her love. But the misery of not knowing if that love were returned had surrounded her ever since.

She allowed herself some comfort in his parting words, assuring her that he would be back. And occasionally she reminded herself that he called her Mrs. Daniels, although that could have been a slip of the tongue. She preferred to think that it wasn't, that he deliberately used the term to reassure her of the reality of their marriage, regardless of its legality. But she didn't know, and the last thing she wanted was false hopes.

No matter how despicable it seemed, Priscilla preferred the truth. If Garth didn't love her, so be it. She would learn to live with that. If only she knew! But that was impossible. He was gone, and there was no knowing when he would be back.

She hoped he wouldn't come while she herself was away, although if he did, Priscilla assumed he would know immediately where to find her. He himself had been the one to tell her of the annual Green Corn Festival in Chota, and he would surely recognize that the season was now upon them.

Straw Basket had been chattering excitedly about it for days, managing at last to arouse some of Priscilla's initial curiosity. By canoe, they would travel to the larger village, where they would stay until the festivities ended, and if Priscilla understood her adoptive sister correctly, they would go to Chota twice more before the year was out. Garth hadn't mentioned the other festivals, yet she felt certain he was far more familiar with the gala events than she.

Prior to her coming, the Aniyv-wiya had collected in the capital town for celebration of the Feast of the New Moon. And since then, local celebrations had accompanied the planting of the corn. On the night before, the villagers had danced to the Old Woman of the Corn, with men and women pouring meal from one basket to another. The next morning, when the planting had begun, the magicians had stomped their feet and chanted prayers for rain. Turtleshell rattles called to the Thunder Man, and bird feathers laid near the stream beckoned to Big Brother Moon.

At the time, Priscilla had thought the customs quaint. She was enamored of Garth and failed to see the significance of the chants, the dance; but now she recognized them for the religious occasions they really were. In fact, she had begun to see how very much of the Aniyv-wiya's life was tied to prayer and praise and other forms of worship. Every act, every chore acknowledged the presence of spiritual beings at work, and Priscilla had no wish to alter the thinking that, she thought, was superior to the acknowledgment of a Sunday-only God.

And yet she felt she had failed in her reasons for coming to this place. She had hoped to share with the people the God of gods, the Light of lights, the Supreme Being who was and is above all others. But how? So far she had merely indicated that such a God did indeed exist, and even then she felt she botched it.

As she looked out over the cloud-obscured mountains, she prayed that God would right this situation, too. Then, reassured that He would, she turned back to the task at hand—getting ready for the trip to Chota. Perhaps the change of scenery would do her good, she thought as she rolled up the garments and packed the few supplies that she would need.

It had been decided that she would travel with White Cloud's family, and so, when Priscilla heard soft footsteps padding into her hut, she assumed Straw Basket had come to fetch her. Looking up from her preparations for the trip, she saw that the girl who had entered her house unannounced was not her adoptive sister.

"Dancing Water! I didn't expect to see you here."

For some reason, the girl had left Priscilla alone since Garth's departure, but now she strode purposefully across the hard-packed dirt floor as though assured of her welcome.

"The trip to Chota is too long," Dancing Water

complained. "You will come with us and say more words from this book." Without hesitation, the girl snatched the Bible from its shelf. Then she glared at Priscilla as though daring her to object.

For an instant, Priscilla reacted with astonishment, then amusement, which she promptly hid. Boredom seemed an odd reason for turning to the Word of God; but the Lord, no doubt, could work through the slightest opening.

"All right," Priscilla agreed. "I'll come with you, if White Cloud doesn't mind. I don't want to offend the family that has been so kind to me."

"I will speak to White Cloud," Dancing Water said, and flounced off apparently to do just that.

Priscilla followed after. The prospect of spending a long canoe ride in the company of Dancing Water was not the way she had wished to spend the day. Of late, she'd had so little time to be with E-tsi and Straw Basket that she had looked forward to some relaxing hours with them on the trip. Yet despite her disappointment, Priscilla thanked God for this unexpected opportunity. Surely it was an answer to her prayer.

"Why do you go with me?" Dancing Water asked when they received White Cloud's approval.

Priscilla didn't hesitate. "Because I think you're an unhappy girl, and the words of the Bible can bring you joy and peace."

Dancing Water frowned. "Do not the words bring love?"

Priscilla couldn't help but smile. "Yes, of course. God is Love, so naturally the words of His Book will bring love. But it's up to you, Dancing Water, to accept the love or refuse it."

The girl nodded thoughtfully. "Bear Claw says the same."

"Bear Claw! You spoke to him about this?"

Dancing Water shrugged.

"Tell me," Priscilla insisted. "What did he say?"

When it looked as though the girl would not comply, Priscilla stopped on the path to the stream. They had neared the low bank where the canoes rested, waiting for the journey to Chota, but Priscilla decided she would not take another step until Dancing Water answered—even if she alone were left behind.

"Are you coming?"

Priscilla shook her head. "Not until you tell me what Bear Claw said."

For a moment the two young women stared at one another, unblinking, as their wills clashed. Finally Dancing Water turned away. "The canoe is ready," she said.

Priscilla didn't answer. Shoulders braced with determination, she wound back up the path from which they'd come. She hadn't gotten far when the girl's shout of "Wait!" halted her.

"My father is the chief," Dancing Water said proudly. "He will not be pleased if you delay him."

Priscilla's smiled at the girl's tactics. "If I do not go with Blazing Sun, then I cannot delay him, can I?"

Dancing Water made a face. "What is it you wish to know?" she asked.

"You tell me."

The girl sighed her displeasure. "Bear Claw says that your Book tells about the Father of All Loves. He says that the Great Spirit is that Father."

"And that's why you want me to read the Bible to you," Priscilla asked, "so that you will know better the Father of All Loves?"

Dancing Water stomped her foot. "The Book has special powers!"

Priscilla's eyes narrowed. "What kind of powers?"

"Do not pretend you do not know!" Dancing Water's animosity flared now, unconcealed. "Bear Claw loves only you. He says that he asked the Father of All Loves to bring you to him, and that is why you are here. He says that the power is so great that he can never love another woman. He is yours for all seasons."

Priscilla closed her eyes against the sudden swell of tears. How very like the Lord to fill her heart with hope when she was most in need of it. She had thought it was impossible to be reassured of Garth's love when he was gone. Yet that reassurance had come—and from the last person she would expected. She chuckled softly.

But Dancing Water misread her chuckle as amusement. "You laugh now, but I will hear the words of the Book. Then I too will have special powers."

"I do not laugh at you, Dancing Water," Priscilla said, opening her eyes. "Come along. Blazing Sun is waiting."

The girl seemed surprised that Priscilla was still willing to read to her, but doing so proved more difficult than either of them had expected. As they rested in the flat bottom of the dug-out, Priscilla had to keep her voice unnaturally low. Even then, her whispered readings were occasionally interrupted by the sharp jab of Dancing Water's elbow when one of the other occupants of the canoe warned them to be quiet. One such interruption lasted so long that Priscilla fell asleep, and later she wondered how she could doze when threatening enemies lurked about.

As they traveled, however, she felt a perfect calm that came from knowing she was in her Father's hands. Clearly He had arranged this time for the sharing of His Word, and Priscilla didn't doubt He would see her through it, regardless of the interruptions.

She decided to start at the beginning because that was usually the best place to begin. If Dancing Water had had prior knowledge of God, the New Testament, perhaps the Book of John, would have been a better place to start. But the girl's concept of myth and magic might make Jesus seem just another god, Priscilla feared. Genesis, she hoped, would leave no doubt about the supremacy of God. All she could do, however, was read. The results were up to Him.

And so she read, "In the beginning, God . . ." until she herself was caught up in the poetry and wonder of the creation account. Although familiar, the passages never failed to move her with fresh understanding and insight—a true mark of the *living* Word. Whether or not Dancing Water was similarly moved, Priscilla didn't know. The girl asked no questions, which seemed odd. It was as though she waited to receive some mystic power without giving even curiosity in return.

Except for her brief nap, Priscilla used the moments of silence to pray. She sought the Lord's counsel for Dancing Water and herself, asking Him to provide her with any explanations needed. Then, when none were required, she read straight through.

She had finished Genesis and enough of Exodus to include the commandments given to Moses when she felt compelled to stop. Her parched throat ached—a sign that she had exceeded her limits—and she didn't believe that God expected her to develop laryngitis by continuing on! He would accept her limitation, even if Dancing Water would not.

"Why do you not tell me more?" the girl complained as soon as Priscilla had closed the leather cover.

"It's not that I don't want to, Dancing Water, but I can't just now."

"So you say." The girl's eyes narrowed suspiciously. "You are afraid I will have more power than you."

"Believe me, nothing would please me more." Priscilla responded sincerely.

A quietening hand cautioned them, and in the silence that followed, Priscilla realized the obvious solution. She would teach Dancing Water to read!

As soon as she could, she told the girl her plan. "Don't you see, it's the perfect answer!" Priscilla exclaimed with such enthusiasm that she was promptly shushed. She lowered her voice to a whisper. "If you will learn to read, Dancing Water, then you will not have to depend on me to read to you."

The girl didn't bother to hide her skepticism. "Why will you do this for me?"

"Because I want you to know the loving God, the Father of all."

Dancing Water gave an uncertain nod.

"Perhaps you'd like it better," Priscilla went on brightly, 'if Straw Basket were included. You could learn to read together. Of course, you'll need to be patient with her since she doesn't know the English language nearly as well as you."

The idea of progressing more rapidly than her cousin seemed to appeal to Dancing Water. This time she nodded briskly. "We will learn today."

Priscilla bit back a smile. "Learning to read may take many days, but it's worth the effort. Once you have learned how, you will know it forever."

"Then I will do this," the girl affirmed.

"You won't be sorry, and—oh! Dancing Water! As I teach you to read, you will also learn how to write down words for yourself. Then other people who can read will see the markings and know what you say."

The girl's eyes widened like black walnuts. "Yes. That, too, is power. We will begin."

"I don't know if we can start the lessons today or not," Priscilla said regretfully. "Remember, I've never been to a festival in Chota, so I don't know what to expect."

"I will tell you."

Priscilla concealed her surprise as Dancing Water, in a low and melodic voice, began to tell her about the Green Corn Festival.

"When the new corn is sweet, the High Chief sends out seven hunters," the girl explained. "The hunters go into the forest to get deer for the feast. One of the hunters wears a mask like the head of a deer. For six days these men remain in the forest.

"The High Chief also sends out messengers," Dancing Water went on. "The messengers go to seven towns and bring back an ear of the new corn from each town. No one picks the corn until then. No one eats it. The messengers call the people of the seven towns to come to the feast. On the night before, the hunters bring in deer; the messengers bring in corn."

"Is that tonight?" interrupted Priscilla.

Dancing Water nodded. "The people will dance the New Green Corn Dance in the town square."

"And tomorrow?"

"Tomorrow you will eat plenty of deer meat and corn," Dancing Water said, laughing, and Priscilla joined her.

The girl's remarks proved true. Throughout the evening, the steady beat of drums kept the people in unison as they danced in an up-down motion, stamping their feet. Priscilla could detect no variation in the simple pattern, but movements of the hands made each dance unique. With a playful quality, the men and women seemed to imitate the world of nature or act out a village scene. But one delightful dance seemed to be a game of follow-the-leader.

Priscilla wondered at their tirelessness. Each step occurred, not by stamping the feet alone, but by lifting and dropping the entire body. Just watching exhausted her, so when Dancing Water told her to try the step, Priscilla declined hastily. "Oh, I can't." And unconsciously she rubbed the imperceptible swell of her abdomen as she spoke.

Dancing Water stared at her intently, her dark eyes growing darker. "Do you carry Bear Claw's child?"

Priscilla compressed her lips. She'd told no one— not even White Cloud or Straw Basket—and it seemed a shame that Dancing Water would be the first to know. Still, she couldn't lie, and so she answered by way of a nod.

"Will you keep my secret to yourself for now?" she pleaded.

The dark eyes gleamed. "I will tell no one," Dancing Water promised.

Instead of relieving Priscilla's mind, however, it gave her a sudden twinge of anxiety. Or was it fear?

She hadn't intended to exclude her adoptive family from the knowledge of her happy news, but Priscilla simply didn't want them making a fuss over her at such an early stage. There was plenty of time, she told herself, and, besides, she rather hoped that Garth would soon return and be the first to know. Now that was no longer possible since Dancing Water had been so quick with her deductions. Too quick?

By the following day the episode was crowded from her mind as preparations for the feast began. The smell of venison drifted about as she joined the others in the council house. From the altar in the center of the room, a fire sparked, and upon it the High Chief laid the seven ears of corn. Priscilla couldn't understand many of the words he chanted, but he appeared to be giving thanks to the Old Woman of the Corn.

This done, the people fell upon the feast, oblivious to the gray eyes watching as Priscilla took it all in. Since arrival, she had been on the lookout for Walkingstick and Little Spoon, but had caught not a glimpse of the medicine man or his apprentice. So many people mulled about that she had difficulty keeping track of her adoptive family and Dancing Water, though that didn't alarm her. Most of the faces were friendly in their solemn way, and a few of the women had sought her out, wanting to touch her hair and skin.

Recognizing one of the women, Priscilla gave a warm smile. Every person was so different from every other that she chided herself for thinking otherwise. The majority of men wore deerskin breechcloths, but some wore shell necklaces, some wore beads, and some tied various kinds of feathers in their scalp lock. Feathers also adorned the weaving, here and there, of women's skirts, and some women wore scarves woven of mulberry bark about their shoulders. Red and black appeared to be the favorite colors, though Priscilla wondered if that was due to the easy accessibility of those dyes.

One woman wore a fringed dress of softest deerskin. Around her trim waist was fastened a wide leather girdle decorated with shells, and above it hung a large medallion, handcrafted in silver. A claw necklace hung from her slender neck, and around her high forehead a beaded strap held two feathers in place. The woman carried a staff, feathered at one end, and both of her wrists were encased in silver. From the wider silver band on the left arm rose the tiered spread of a white wing, halted in flight.

Priscilla had wondered how she would recognize Nan-ye-hi, and now she knew. Not only was the woman's dress unmistakably regal, but so was her bearing. Taller than most of the women, her queenly posture dignified her honored position, and even more majestic was her beauty. She had no need for the reddish paint that was often worn cosmetically, for the natural tint of her skin was the pinkish hue of the silky wild rose. Indeed, before the feast was over, Priscilla heard someone call the woman by her appropriate name.

Seeing the Beloved Woman now, Priscilla realized how presumptuous she had been in hoping for a word with her. Really, she had nothing to discuss— nothing specific, that is. She had merely wanted to draw from the courage and wisdom of this outstanding person. It was with tremendous surprise, then, that she realized Nan-ye-hi was returning her stare.

Slowly, gracefully, the woman approached her, her large black eyes piercing Priscilla's own gray ones. Then, holding out a hand in a gesture of peace and friendship, Nan-ye-hi smiled, instantly transforming the regal face into one of incredible kindness.

"Welcome, Mourning Dove."

"You—you know me."

The smile deepened. "How could I not know you when Walkingstick and Little Spoon tell me of your courage?" The beautiful face grew more serious. "You will need much bravery to remain long in this land, Mourning Dove. Troubles come from far and near, from your people and from mine. We must speak to them the words of truth until they listen. We must show them that both peoples have much to learn."

"I couldn't agree with you more, Nan-ye-hi. Tell me what to do, and I will follow your counsel."

The lovely smile returned. "You are young, Mourning Dove, but the Great Spirit gives you wisdom. To me, he says, teach my people the white man's ways of farming and raising livestock. To you, the Great Spirit gives other instructions, but you will know. Bear Claw says you hear E-do-da's voice."

"You have seen Bear Claw recently?" Priscilla asked, her heart thumping at the mention of his name.

"It has been two moons or more. He did not remain long in Chota."

"Do you know where he was going? Or when he will return?"

"I cannot say, but he travels like the eagle toward the rising sun."

"East?" Priscilla queried, dismayed. "He didn't tell me that he was going back East so soon." And now that she knew, Priscilla dreaded the lapse of more weeks before his return. Her spirits sank.

"Be not troubled, Mourning Dove, about Bear Claw," Nan-ye-hi said. "He is with you even now. But you must be wary of serpents. Give kindness to all in equal measure. And do not let your enemies deceive you."

Thinking about the conversation later, Priscilla realized how unusual it was, although she had expected no less from the Beloved Woman. Nan-ye-hi spoke with almost prophetic wisdom. Yet even so, it did not occur to Priscilla that she had anything to fear.

## CHAPTER 12

IN THE WEEKS FOLLOWING the Green Corn Festival, the reading lessons progressed remarkably well. As anticipated, Dancing Water proved to be the quicker student since her command of the English language and her strong motivation kept her going when Straw Basket was ready to quit.

Some days Priscilla would have preferred a shortened lesson. When she had suggested the idea of reading lessons, she did not realize how taxing it would be, bending over with a thickened waist to scratch letters and short words in the dirt. But she couldn't give up when Dancing Water was so eager, and not when the only book available was the precious copy of God's Word.

It was Priscilla's fondest hope that the message itself would stir up Dancing Water's mind and heart, giving the girl a true desire to learn about God. Dancing Water had not mentioned again her wish for greater power, and Priscilla was encouraged that the spirit of the Gospel was beginning to take hold.

Straw Basket, however, with her faltering speech and labored pronunciations, was the one who began asking questions, and Priscilla rejoiced in the interest shown by her adoptive sister. The Book of Psalms had proven a particular favorite, and after one such passage, Straw Basket looked up quizzically.

"This God has made all that there is, and yet He speaks to His people."

"That's right," Priscilla said. "And if you but ask Him, Straw Basket, He will speak to *you*."

"How will I know this?"

Priscilla leaned against a stout oak, her weary back glad for the respite as she thought how to answer Straw Basket's question. In the distance rumbled the waterfall, for the three women had agreed to have their instructions in this favored spot.

"First, there's the law," Priscilla responded at last, while her sister listened intently. "Remember, we read the commandments that God gave to Moses in one of our lessons. Well, those laws are for us, too, and nothing God says will conflict with them."

"Conflict?"

"Go against them," Priscilla explained. "But God's Word is not only law, it is love, and if we want to know the way of love, the truth of love, the life of love, then we must look at God's Son, Jesus.

"But there's a problem," Priscilla went on. "No matter how hard we try, we cannot possibly be as kind or as loving as God. Someone has to pay for our mistakes, and so God sent His own Son to do it. Actually, you could say He sent Himself."

"I do not understand," Straw Basket admitted.

"Nor do I," Priscilla said. "It's too wonderful to understand completely. But we can believe that it happened, that part of God became a man named Jesus, simply because His love for us was so great."

"He would do this for me?"

Priscilla smiled. "He *did* do it for you, Straw Basket. And He would have done so even if you were the only person on earth."

"And this Jesus. Does He still live?"

"He died, yet He lives again. It is Jesus who will speak to you now. He will comfort you when you are sad. He will encourage you when you feel disheartened. He will teach you what you need to know when the time is right. But He will never deceive you, He will never lie to you, and He will never accuse you or make you feel bad about yourself or other people. You can trust Him, Straw Basket, for He is perfect love."

"Where will I find Him?"

"Everywhere. But mostly in the people who open themselves to His love."

"Then I will speak with Him." Straw Basket spoke so decisively that Priscilla had no doubts her sister meant it.

What a beautiful day that was, Priscilla thought later, with even the surroundings contributing to its glory! The cool spray of the waterfall fanned the crisp autumn air, and a choir of birds spanned the cathedral ceiling of yellow oak and red maple leaves. Acorns and an occasional pecan tithed their offerings, and late-blooming black-eyed susans adorned the altars of mountain rock.

Only the attitude of Dancing Water had shrouded the bright moment, and Priscilla prayed that nothing would act as a stumblingblock to hinder the girl's progress. Although she was reading exceptionally well for such a short time of instruction, she gave no indication that she comprehended the readings. Only once, in fact, did Priscilla perceive special interest on Dancing Water's part, and that was when they'd read the fourth verse of the eighty-ninth Psalm: "Thy seed will I establish forever." Oddly, Priscilla recalled, the girl had frowned.

Generally, however, Dancing Water reacted impassively, her enthusiasm reserved for the task itself, although Priscilla couldn't help but notice that the girl sought her out more and, in her own way, tried to be of assistance.

"Your back hurts," Dancing Water commented at the end of one particularly lengthy lesson. "I will make a soothing tea."

"Why, thank you," Priscilla exclaimed, delighted that the girl had exhibited this measure of unexpected caring. She chose to ignore the odd tone in her voice.

Rather thick for tea, the beverage tasted good, sweetened as it was with wild berries, and Priscilla expressed her appreciation even more profusely. Dancing Water seemed pleased.

"I will make it for you each day," she promised.

Accepting this hospitality, Priscilla had to laugh. It was rather like the time she brought Mammy Sue's pecan fudge to her tutor, hoping to win favor. Apparently Dancing Water sensed the strong attachment between her own tutor and Straw Basket and hoped somehow to gain more attention for herself. Well, Priscilla thought, there was no harm in that. After their lessons, Straw Basket preferred to get back to her weaving, and Priscilla supposed the extra moments alone with Dancing Water were well-spent.

The girl had not mentioned Garth again, which

made their private times more companionable. Priscilla missed him dreadfully. She hoped he would return before the first flutterings of the baby's movements, for she was certain he would be as excited about it as she. Once or twice she felt a ripping sensation across her abdomen, which she thought might be their child astir, but she wasn't sure. Perhaps she even wanted to postpone that moment for Garth to share, yet by doing so she failed to share it with her loved ones at hand.

Since Dancing Water was still the only soul to know Priscilla's secret, she was the one in whom the mother-to-be confided one afternoon. They ended lessons early because of Priscilla's discomfort, which Straw Basket attributed to a stomach ache. She had seen Priscilla to the hut, then left her there, having extracted from her a promise to rest. And obligingly Priscilla had closed her eyes. But a sharp contraction caused them to fly open once again. As she looked frantically about, Dancing Water appeared in the doorway.

"Oh, I'm glad to see you! Something's wrong, I think."

Quickly the girl prepared the sweet beverage that Priscilla had come to like, but now she pushed the tea away.

"I don't think I can drink anything," Priscilla apologized.

"You must," Dancing Water commanded. "Here. Drink this while I gather roots for you. Then you will never have these pains again."

The girl's soothing promise failed to comfort, however, as Priscilla gasped beneath a thrusting pain. Although she did sip the sweet liquid, her deepest instincts told her to get up, to seek White Cloud's aid. But her body could not comply. The pains had worsened—so intensely that Priscilla found it impossible to walk. Beads of perspiration adorned her forehead.

The beverage done little good by the time Dancing Water returned, and Priscilla felt queasy.

"The pain is worse—much worse. Please bring White Cloud to me."

"I will," the girl agreed. "But you must chew this root and swallow it. Then I will bring White Cloud."

With no one else to aid her, Priscilla did as told.

"Do you feel better?" asked Dancing Water in a voice no longer benign.

"I—I feel dizzy. What's happening to me?" Priscilla asked. But she never heard the answer.

When she awoke, White Cloud was kneeling over her, stroking her forehead with a cool cloth. The scent of herbal water reached Priscilla's nose, but only a whiff, for the overpowering smell was one of death. No words were needed as her eyes, large with pain and fright, searched E-tsi's face. The older woman shook her head sadly and laid a gentle hand on Priscilla's abdomen.

Priscilla thought her heart would break. This child whom Garth had wanted most dearly, whom she had loved so well, was not meant to be. *No!* Priscilla told herself. That wasn't true! God was the Father of love, the creator of life. He was certainly not responsible for the death of her child, even if He had permitted it to happen. Besides, had He not warned her? Did He not speak to her through Nan-ye-hi? Priscilla railed against herself. If only she had understood the message . . . .

No. That was the voice of the accuser, Priscilla knew, and not God. Yet guilt deepened her grief in the following days until she asked the Lord to help her forgive herself for being such a fool. Then, as she prayed, it seemed incredible that she could have trusted her baby's life, and even her own, to a girl who wished her nothing but harm. For Priscilla was coming to suspect a terrible truth—that what had proven fatal to the child was the lovely "tea" and the root. She shuddered thinking about it.

To her relief, she caught no glimpse of Dancing Water as she lay abed, recuperating. At first she wanted to lash out, to tell everyone what she suspected the girl had done, but no good purpose would be served. She kept quiet, which at last brought Dancing Water to her door.

"You have not spoken ill against me," the girl said as she stood in the entranceway to the hut.

"Would it bring back my baby?" Priscilla asked, chilled.

When Dancing Water did not respond, Priscilla coaxed her into answering the one question she wanted most to know: "Why?"

"I did not try to kill you," the girl responded at last with a haughty snap of her head. "It was the child, which your Book told me I must not allow, or the seed of you and Bear Claw would be established forever."

"How dare you use the Bible for your own selfish purposes!" Priscilla exclaimed, though she knew it wasn't the first time such a dreadful thing had happened.

Priscilla sighed. She supposed she was negligent in not telling the girl about the presence of another power—a lesser, but evil power, and now she did so briefly.

"You must be careful, Dancing Water," she went on to explain, "to shut out the voice of the evil one. It will bring you no good, and the Great Spirit within you will get smaller and smaller until it no longer exists. My words are not meant to frighten you, Dancing Water. But you must decide which power you will follow—the greater or the lesser, the good or the ill. It's up to you."

For a moment Dancing Water said nothing, contenting herself to stare at some unseen object on the floor. Then she burst out, "The hemlock root you chewed was meant for other seed, too."

"What?"

"You heard," the girl said defiantly. "But you must chew and swallow the root for four days before all seed will die. I gave you too much. I will not have your blood upon me!" Dancing Water declared, then rushed away.

Sickened, Priscilla lay back down and closed her eyes. She couldn't have understood Dancing Water correctly, could she? Yes, the girl *had* admitted that Priscilla's suspicions were true; the thick tea was indeed responsible for the death of the unborn child, simply by bringing it far too prematurely into the world. But the malice didn't end there, Priscilla realized now. The hemlock root that Dancing Water had given her to chew and swallow was not meant to poison her. It was part of a treatment—a murderous attempt on all of the children Priscilla had yet to conceive!

Had the hemlock worked? Was all future seed now dead, poisoned by a poisoning spirit of hate and covetousness? Dancing Water had said the treatment for such sterility required four days to succeed, and knowing that much time was not available, she merely increased the dose. Apparently the girl became frightened when she thought Priscilla herself would die, and so she had fetched White Cloud after all. Priscilla lived. But was all hope of a family dead?

Now unanswerable, the question tormented her. She could neither eat nor sleep, thinking about it, and her daily chores were soon forgotten. Stale water sat about in a clay pot, collecting dirt, and the ashes on the fire went cold, while Priscilla didn't care. She didn't even notice.

She began taking long, aimless walks into the forest, alone, unmindful of her safety. Garth would be better off without her, she decided. Even though he loved her—*because* he loved her—she didn't want to bring to him a fruitless marriage. He deserved more, needed more.

Without realizing where she wandered one day, Priscilla ventured along the path that led her to the waterfall. The thunderous spray burst upon her reverie as she saw where her treacherous footsteps had taken her. This was the place of solitude she had loved. This was the place she had first realized her love for Garth, where he had asked her to marry him. This was the place where she had painstakingly scratched out the letters of the alphabet, where she had told Straw Basket about a living God, a loving Savior. And this was the place where Dancing Water's evil scheme had been conceived.

The stick she used to scratch the dirt lay discarded now against a boulder, and Priscilla snatched it up as though it were a serpent. With furious loathing, she beat and beat the stick of wood against the rock until it split and splintered. Gone were the lessons. Gone were the dreams. Gone were the angry tears she had stored in bitterness. She wept, and her sobs broke louder than the thundering falls.

"O God, I can't go on like this!" she cried. Then the intensity of her anger and hatred toward Dancing Water frightened her, and she sat down on the rock, subdued.

She hated the girl—she admitted it—and she never wanted to see her again. Yet even knowing she was justified in her feelings toward Dancing Water brought no comfort. But were such feelings ever justified? Shivering, she wrapped her arms around herself. Somehow the hatred had to stop; somehow she had to break its hold upon her.

There was no way of knowing right now if Dancing Water had succeeded in her malevolent mission. But neither was there any way of knowing if Priscilla had succeeded in her mission of benevolence and love. In the final revelation of the matter, which force would overcome, good or ill? And which, Priscilla wondered, would she herself represent? As long as this awful hatred had its hold. . . .

She shuddered. Dancing Water's actions were murderous, but so were her own reactions.

"Heavenly Father, Lord of all, I need Your saving power. I could murder, too," Priscilla choked out in prayer. "Forgive me, Lord. And Father, I *choose* to ask You to help me forgive Dancing Water. Send Your saving grace upon us, and let the overcoming be in Christ's name. Amen."

She blinked. Incredibly, God's response was instantaneous, for Priscilla had already drawn the first peaceful breath she had had in days. A calmness, inside and outside of herself, prevailed, and she knew beyond a doubt that whatever happened, it would be all right. With the hatred and unforgiveness removed, God was again with her. No, He had been there all along, but choked off by darkness, her spirit had been unable to receive Him. Prayer had loosed her from the clutches of all that would harm her in body, mind, or spirit.

It was then she realized she had no business being in the forest alone, and she thanked God for protecting her—not only her, but Garth. Whatever would it do to him to have her, too, torn apart by a bear or some other wild creature?

Hurriedly, she scrambled down the path to the village. Soon dusk would fall, with only the spark of a fire and the sediment-ridden water to see her through the night. She hurried along, stopping only to grab pieces of firewood that lay here and there beside the path. Even those, she thought, must be providentially supplied.

Priscilla was so intent on completing her belated chores that she didn't notice the girl in the field until she came quite near. When she saw it was Dancing Water, she supposed she could turn around or change her course, but at the same moment it occurred to her that God's timing was at work. She wouldn't be surprised if He had actually planned their meeting.

Maintaining her pace, Priscilla approached the girl warily. She could not—would not—pretend a liking for Dancing Water, but neither did she wish the girl ill any longer. Praise God for that, she thought, for it certainly was not of her own doing.

A few steps away, she struggled with what she would say. And then, suddenly, the healing words were there.

"God be with you, Dancing Water."

Priscilla did not pause, in word or step, but the greeting had its desired effect. Both Dancing Water and Priscilla knew that the girl was forgiven.

Dusk fell on a rekindled hearth, and when Priscilla slept, she rested more peacefully than she had since Garth's departure. It would take time to heal her body completely; time to ease the grief of losing a child; time to convince and convict Dancing Water of a loving God. But knowing He did not slumber, she could rest. And when she awoke, Garth was there.

Priscilla stretched. "I must be dreaming!"

"A nightmare is more like it," Garth said, scooping her into his arms. "I wish you had told me you were expecting a child. God forgive me for not being here when you needed me."

"Darling, you mustn't blame yourself," Priscilla said, her soft lips brushing his pinched face. "You thought I would be safe in the village, and I would have been if I'd heeded Nan-ye-hi's warning and not allowed myself to be deceived."

"I don't understand." He pulled away, his dark eyes tormented and confused. "When White Cloud told me you lost the baby, I assumed you had overdone. Now don't look at me that way, Priscilla. I know you're not made of porcelain, but neither are you cast in bronze."

She allowed herself the hint of a smile before she sighed. Garth would have to know the truth, yet she feared for his own safety. Dancing Water would never harm him physically, of course, but how much harm would the girl do to his spirit if he refused to forgive her? God only knew.

Priscilla shut her eyes as she asked the Lord to guide her in telling Garth what had happened. And then the words flowed as she lovingly explained, her eyes now meeting his.

"You could blame her," Priscilla finished, "but what good would it do? It wouldn't bring back the baby. And you could blame yourself for not being here. Or you could blame me for being such a—a simpleton! But I hope you won't do any of those things, Garth. I hope you'll ask God to forgive—her, you, me—all of us."

"Good grief, Priscilla. Do you know what you're asking?" Then, seeing the pain in her gray eyes, he quieted. "Yes, I guess you do know."

Rising, he paced the room. And when he halted, his dark eyes glistened with tears. "Why? Can you tell me that? Why did this have to happen?"

"I don't know," Priscilla admitted. "I've asked, but it did no good. Garth, please let go of it. We must ask God to help us forgive even Him, if need be! If you feel as I did, you probably don't want to do even that. But it's a choice. Forgiveness is a choice."

His shoulders slumped wearily. "How? What do I do?" he asked. Then, for the first time since their wedding ceremony, they agreed in prayer. God would forgive and be forgiven. God would heal. God would bring good out of evil.

When the prayer ended, Garth gathered Priscilla in a tight embrace. "I love you, Little Dove," he whispered.

Wryly, she smiled. "It was Dancing Water who convinced me of that."

He grimaced. "I suppose I should be grateful. I didn't know how to convince you myself. Do you

170

realize how difficult it is to prove you love someone?" he added thoughtfully.

Priscilla gave a laugh. "Indeed I do! I knew I had fallen in love with you that day by the waterfall, but it was too soon to tell you. You would never have believed me then."

"We'll never know, will we?" He tipped her face to catch the morning light filtering through the hole in the thatched roof. "But, Little Dove, I loved you from the moment you opened those big gray velvet eyes and set your lashing tongue on me. You had the spirited strength to match your beauty, and as soon as you met Straw Basket, I knew you were loving, too. You had been through a shock, and yet you handled yourself with intelligence and humor. And as I came to know you, I saw that your gentility was tempered with a giving nature that you couldn't hide. What more could a man ask for, Priscilla? You were, quite literally, the answer to a prayer. But then I couldn't believe God had actually done it. I kept thinking it was all a mistake, and you would leave as soon as you found out."

"Oh, Garth! Is that why you led me to believe you were a judge?"

He nodded grimly. "I couldn't bear to see you go."

"Nor I, you."

"Forgive me for not trusting you or God to work out the matter, for not having enough faith in His love or ours. And then, when it *did* work, I thought you only wanted to use me."

"You know I love you," Priscilla said softly.

"Until this happened," Garth went on, "I never realized how much fear can destroy faith. That in itself is rather frightening."

Priscilla bit her lip, nodding. "I'm afraid now, Garth."

"Of what?" he asked gently.

She looked at the floor, drew a deep breath and let it out with the words, "That we'll never have the family you so wanted."

Garth pulled her chin up firmly until she again looked him in the eyes. "Priscilla Daniels, you *are* my family! Don't you know that?"

"But Garth—"

"No but's. We'll take what comes—together—you and I and God."

Her dimpled chin quivered in his loving hand. "Then we're back where we started—with no more means of having a proper ceremony than we had a few months ago. Don't misunderstand me, Garth," she added quickly. "In my mind, we are as married as two people can be . . . ."

"More."

"All right—more." She smiled fleetingly. "But if we had come here to live and not had a ceremony acceptable to the Aniyv-wiya, that would have been offensive. And if we live elsewhere without a legal ceremony, that too would be offensive. Love doesn't offend," she ended simply.

"Nor does it *take* offense easily," Garth added wryly. "Perhaps you'll remember that, too. Nevertheless, there's nothing for you to worry your pretty little head about, Priscilla." Folding his arms across his chest, Garth looked at her with a smile. "Do you recall, per chance, a Reverend Jones?"

Priscilla's lips parted, but for a moment no sound came out. "Is—is that why you traveled east? To fetch him?"

Garth laughed. "Or any other minister of God who would agree to accompany me. But it was the good reverend I found, and not too far from your home."

"You went without me!"

"Don't fret, Little Dove. We'll go back soon."

Priscilla's eyes narrowed. "Garth Daniels! You were afraid if you took me with you, I wouldn't come back," she accused him, and he did not deny it. "And here I thought you didn't want me to be part of your family or you of mine! I thought you'd accept me only if I were truly part of the Wolf Clan." Lightly she touched the jagged scar, pink against his cheek.

"Silly Priscilla," he said, so tenderly she didn't mind. "Neither of us, it seems, has had reason to fear that our commitment was genuine. It is, you know." Then he looked exceptionally pleased with himself. "And you'll be happy to learn that I've succeeded in gaining your father's blessings."

"Oh, Garth!" she said, her large eyes even wider. "How on earth did you manage that?"

"I expect it wasn't earthly powers that triumphed," he admitted. "Your father proved as difficult to convince as you. All he wanted to know was that you were cared for and cherished, Priscilla. He loves you very much."

She nodded, teary-eyed. 'Sometimes he has an odd way of showing it."

"Don't we all," Garth said, drawing her close, his lips brushing the top of her silken hair. "You'll be glad to know, however, that the Lord provided me with an ally from the start."

Priscilla tipped back her head. "Who?"

"Your sister, of course. For some reason she took an immediate liking to me and sized up the situation rather astutely."

"Lettie?"

Garth gave a dry laugh. "You needn't be so stunned. I can behave nicely—except when I'm with you," he added smiling.

Priscilla stilled his distracting hands. "Garth, are you saying that Lettie actually approved of you? Approved of our marriage?"

"Why shouldn't she? I made it clear to her that I love you, and she could readily see why you're equally smitten with me," he teased.

"Oh." Suddenly Priscilla felt ashamed.

"You're thinking of Charles," Garth said, serious now. "Lettie was upset with you for going off with him when there was no deep love between the two of you, Priscilla, but I think she understands now your reasons. She admits she was rather hard on you."

"I deserved it. Oh, Garth, Charles' family! Did you—"

"They know. Naturally they were distressed to hear of his death, but oddly enough they didn't seem surprised," he added. "It relieved them greatly to know you were well—and loved."

"I'd like to tell them that his bringing me here has already born fruit," Priscilla said wistfully. She told Garth then about the reading lessons and Straw Basket's acceptance of the loving Father made manifest in Christ. "I still have hopes for Dancing Water, too," she ended shyly.

Garth sighed. "So have I—but only because God can work miracles."

Priscilla smiled. "He's certainly revealed a number of them today! Oh, Garth, I'm so pleased my family likes you. And Lettie! I never dreamed she would approve."

"Perhaps," Garth drawled, "she's presently inclined to discern a romance when she sees one. She's getting married herself soon."

"Lettie? Married?" Priscilla exclaimed. "To whom?"

"A young man who's just come over from England, I believe. Nice fellow. He and Lettie seemed quite taken with each other."

"But she said she would never marry. She said she'd take care of Mama, and . . .Garth! Is my mother—?"

"She's fine. As well as ever, that is, and you've no cause to worry. Lettie will still see to her. Although I must admit, it's plain that your sister has difficulty remembering that others are around when her Lord Chaucey is present." He chuckled.

"Lord Chaucey? From England, you said?"

Garth nodded, and to his surprise, Priscilla burst into giggles.

"Have I missed something?"

"No," Priscilla laughed. "I have. Papa fetched him for me. Now don't pout, Garth! It's worked out rather well, don't you think? My father never would have set out to make a match for Lettie. And it seems," she said, snuggling close, "that I've done just fine for myself."

"So have I," he answered. "We truly are blessed, Little Dove."

"I know."

The kiss she had waited for in solitude came swiftly and lightly, its feathery touch stroking, coaxing the beat of her heart. Contented, Priscilla sighed. Then she caught her breath as Garth's lips pressed harder, more demanding, against hers.

"Oh, I love you, Little Dove," he said, his voice muffled against the hollow of her throat.

His name became her breath as she quivered beneath his touch. "I love you, Garth—completely."

Suddenly he was pulling her to her feet. "I'm going to make you a respectable woman." He kissed her forehead then with his dark eyes looked lovingly into hers.

"Get dressed, Priscilla darling," he commanded. "The Reverend Jones is waiting."

## EPILOGUE

IN THE SAME YEAR of their marriage, 1773, Garth's prediction that the colonists would eventually tire of having no say in their government came true. On December 16, a group of protestors dumped tea in Boston Harbor. Upon hearing of the matter, Garth laughed. He was not amused that the colonists wanted to elect their own officials, as the Aniyv-Wiya had had the privilege of doing, but he chuckled over the disguise that the colonists had used for the occasion. Hoping to lay blame elsewhere, the men had dressed themselves as Indians, not realizing perhaps how ridiculous a choice they had made.

By the time the news of the incident reached the region of the Smoky Mountains, Dancing Water was living in Chota, having married a distant relative of Bryant Ward. Since Priscilla was by then traveling with Garth, she never saw the girl again. Yet she included her in her prayers, remembering her especially when she mourned the absence of her child.

Although Priscilla and Garth felt they were complete together, their family did eventually grow. Lettie was the first, however, to present her parents with a grandchild, a son; and after his birth, Mrs. Davis was coaxed by the infant's wails out of the enveloping cloak of withdrawal. She was, in fact, almost like the person Priscilla had known from her early childhood when they returned home, at Garth's insistence, after the birth of their own baby girl.

Straw Basket, who had not married, dubbed her blond-haired, brown-eyed niece Corn Tassel, a fitting name that Garth promptly shortened to Tassie.

The following year, a son entered the world with a thatch of black on his head and a pair of enormous gray eyes that took in everything as he swung from his cradleboard. Priscilla and Garth agreed that the child should be called Charles Davis, but somehow neither name stuck. And so it was Chad who later roamed the woods with his pleased papa, and who asked again and again to hear the stories of the bear—and how his father had won.

## ABOUT THE AUTHOR

MARY HARWELL SAYLER has long been interested in Native Americans—even before she realized her great, great, great, great-grandmother was a member of the Cherokee nation. Historical romances have long been favorites too, and Mary hopes this is the second of many she is to write. She also writes children's books and poetry and, in her *un*spare time, instructs beginning writers through correspondence study with the Christian Writers' Fellowship. It's only natural then, that after devoloping a series on poetry-writing for CWF, Mary wrote two study units on writing the romance novel.

Look for her contemporary romance, CANDLE, to be published soon.

# A Letter To Our Readers

Dear Reader:

In order that we might better contribute to your reading enjoyment, we would appreciate your taking a few minutes to respond to the following questions and return to:

> Editor, Serenade Books
> The Zondervan Publishing House
> 1415 Lake Drive, S.E.
> Grand Rapids, Michigan  49506

1. Did you enjoy reading BEYOND THE SMOKY CURTAIN?

☐ Very much. I would like to see more books by this author!
☐ Moderately
☐ I would have enjoyed it more if _____

2. Where did you purchase this book? _____

3. What influenced your decision to purchase this book?

☐ Cover                    ☐ Back cover copy
☐ Title                    ☐ Friends
☐ Publicity                ☐ Other _____

4. Would you be interested in reading other Serenade/Serenata or Serenade/Saga Books?

☐ Very interested
☐ Moderately interested
☐ Not interested

5. Please indicate your age range:

☐ Under 18    ☐ 25–34    ☐ 46–55
☐ 18–24       ☐ 35–45    ☐ Over 55

6. Would you be interested in a Serenade book club? If so, please give us your name and address:

Name _____

Occupation _____

Address _____

City _____ State _____ Zip _____

*Serenade Saga* books are inspirational romances in historical settings, designed to bring you a joyful, heart-lifting reading experience.

*Serenade Saga* books available in your local book store:

#1 SUMMER SNOW, Sandy Dengler
#2 CALL HER BLESSED, Jeanette Gilge
#3 INA, Karen Baker Kletzing
#4 JULIANA OF CLOVER HILL,
    Brenda Knight Graham
#5 SONG OF THE NEREIDS, Sandy Dengler
#6 ANNA'S ROCKING CHAIR,
    Elaine Watson
#7 IN LOVE'S OWN TIME,
    Susan C. Feldhake
#8 YANKEE BRIDE, Jane Peart
#9 LIGHT OF MY HEART, Kathleen Karr
#10 LOVE BEYOND SURRENDER,
    Susan C. Feldhake
#11 ALL THE DAYS AFTER SUNDAY,
    Jeannette Gilge
#12 WINTERSPRING, Sandy Dengler
#13 HAND ME DOWN THE DAWN,
    Mary Harwell Sayler
#14 REBEL BRIDE, Jane Peart
#15 SPEAK SOFTLY, LOVE, Kathleen Yapp
#16 FROM THIS DAY FORWARD, Kathleen Karr
#17 THE RIVER BETWEEN, Jacquelyn Cook
#18 VALIANT BRIDE, Jane Peart
#19 WAIT FOR THE SUN, Maryn Langer
#20 KINCAID OF CRIPPLE CREEK, Peggy Darty

*Serenade Serenata* books are inspirational romances in contemporary settings, designed to bring you a joyful, heart-lifting reading experience.

*Serenade Serenata* books available in your local bookstore:

Watch for other books in both the *Serenade Saga* (historical) and *Serenade Serenata* (contemporary) series coming soon.